"Megan…" Gage paused to clear his throat, probably of the words that were sticking there.

No matter that they each had their own reasons for agreeing to this arrangement, to actually propose would be a mockery of the special moment that every girl—even the geeky ones—dreamed of. And Megan couldn't let that happen.

"Yes," she said, giving him the answer he needed without waiting for the question neither of them wanted to hear him ask.

His relief was almost palpable as he took the ring out of the box and slid it on her finger. Then he exhaled audibly and rose to his feet.

She stared at the diamond cluster that somehow seemed even larger—and felt a lot heavier—on her hand. She swallowed. "I guess that makes it official."

Dear Reader,

I've always enjoyed reading and writing connected stories because of the opportunities they provide to meet new characters and revisit old friends.

A few years ago I wrote a book called *The Marriage Solution*. It was, at the time, a stand-alone story, but the hero had a brother, and even then I knew that I would write his story someday.

Of course, Gage Richmond was an unapologetic playboy who had some growing up to do before he was worthy of his own happily-ever-after. Thankfully, Megan Roarke is just the right woman to help him on that journey.

I'm thrilled to share their story with you and excited to announce that *The Engagement Project* is only the first book in my new BRIDES & BABIES miniseries from Silhouette Special Edition. Because I've always enjoyed meeting new characters and revisiting old friends. ☺

I hope you enjoy reading their story as much as I enjoyed writing it.

All the best,

Brenda Harlen

THE ENGAGEMENT PROJECT

BRENDA HARLEN

Silhouette®

SPECIAL EDITION®

Published by Silhouette Books

America's Publisher of Contemporary Romance

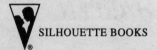 **SILHOUETTE BOOKS**

Recycling programs
for this product may
not exist in your area.

ISBN-13: 978-0-373-65503-8

THE ENGAGEMENT PROJECT

Copyright © 2010 by Brenda Harlen

Visit Silhouette Books at www.eHarlequin.com

Printed in U.S.A.

Books by Brenda Harlen

Silhouette Special Edition

Once and Again #1714
*Her Best-Kept Secret #1756
The Marriage Solution #1811
†One Man's Family #1827
The New Girl in Town #1859
**The Prince's Royal Dilemma #1898
**The Prince's Cowgirl Bride #1920
††Family in Progress #1928
**The Prince's Holiday Baby #1942
*‡The Texas Tycoon's
    Christmas Baby* #2016
‡‡The Engagement Project #2021

Silhouette Romantic Suspense

McIver's Mission #1224
Some Kind of Hero #1246
Extreme Measures #1282
Bulletproof Hearts #1313
Dangerous Passions #1394

*Family Business
†Logan's Legacy Revisited
**Reigning Men
††Back in Business
‡The Foleys and the McCords
‡‡Brides and Babies

BRENDA HARLEN

grew up in a small town surrounded by books and imaginary friends. Although she always dreamed of being a writer, she chose to follow a more traditional career path first. After two years of practicing as an attorney (including an appearance in front of the Supreme Court of Canada), she gave up her "real" job to be a mom and to try her hand at writing books. Three years, five manuscripts and another baby later, she sold her first book—an RWA Golden Heart winner—to Silhouette Books.

Brenda lives in southern Ontario with her real-life husband/hero, two heroes-in-training and two neurotic dogs. She is still surrounded by books ("too many books," according to her children) and imaginary friends, but she also enjoys communicating with "real" people. Readers can contact Brenda by e-mail at brendaharlen@yahoo.com or by snail mail c/o Silhouette Books, 233 Broadway, Suite 1001, New York, NY 10279.

To my mom—
Because you taught me to be strong,
to believe in myself and to never give up.
And because there's a little bit of you
in every one of my heroines.
I love you.

Chapter One

Megan Roarke hated shopping.

Her older sister often teased that there was something defective in Megan's double-X chromosome that she balked at going to the mall. Of course, Megan couldn't expect her to understand. Ashley was "the beautiful one"—the one who looked good in anything and drew glances of admiration wherever she went.

Megan, on the other hand, had always been referred to as "the smart one." She'd started to read when she was three years old and had spent most of the next twenty years with her nose in a book. She read everything she could get her hands on—from fantastical stories about magical lands to biographies of world leaders to technical manuals. Books were her bridges to so many different places, knowledge was the key that opened new worlds—and a whole lot of other clichés that hid the real truth: she'd been a painfully shy and socially inept child who found refuge from the harsh realities of life between the covers of a book.

And through her reading, she'd learned that the childhood labels attached to herself and her sister did both of them a disservice. While Ashley was undeniably beautiful, she was also a smart and savvy woman; and though Megan accepted that there would always be people who were intimidated by her high IQ, she knew her intelligence wasn't the sum total of her character.

Still, she didn't bother to try and dispel the stereotypical image people inevitably formed when they learned that she was a scientist, because she *was* a lab geek. She loved her work, and she would much rather spend time with formulas than people. Not that she disliked people, exactly. She just didn't understand them. Elemental properties were consistent and chemical reactions were predictable. Human beings, on the other hand, always seemed *in*consistent and *un*predictable.

Ashley claimed that was what made people so interesting, and she would know. Not only had Megan's sister enjoyed an active social life before she'd met the man who was now her fiancé, she taught first grade at a local school and absolutely thrived in the environment of incessant noise and unending chaos that was created by twenty six-year-olds in a classroom.

But it was the recent engagement that was the cause of Megan's dreaded trip to the Pinehurst Shopping Center. Apparently it wasn't enough that Trevor had put a ring on Ashley's finger, now they were having a party to celebrate the event.

"Nothing fancy," Ashley had assured her. "Just drinks and hors d'oeuvres with family and some close friends."

Of course, Megan knew her sister's definition of "nothing fancy" was drastically different from her own and that even drinks and hors d'oeuvres required something a little more formal than comfy faded jeans and her favorite "Go Green" T-shirt—especially since their mother had become involved in the planning.

The sky had turned dark by the time Megan pulled into a vacant parking space and the first drops of rain were starting to fall as she dashed across the lot.

The mall was busier than she would have expected for a Friday afternoon, and she found herself hesitating inside the entrance.

She'd always been a little uncomfortable in crowds, always feeling as if everyone was looking at her. It wasn't just an irrational feeling but a ridiculous one, because the reality was that no one ever noticed her. Megan didn't stand out in a crowd of one, but she still had to force herself to take a deep breath before she could step forward.

For a lot of years, she'd simply avoided crowds rather than fight against the panicky feelings they stirred inside. But over the past few years, she'd made an effort to overcome this fear, and had mostly done so. She rarely felt afraid anymore, just awkward and uncomfortable.

A strand of hair had come loose from her ponytail and she tucked it behind her ear as she studied the mall directory, looking for Chaundra's Boutique.

"I asked Anne-Marie to set aside the cutest little dress that I know will look fabulous on you," Ashley had told her.

Nothing had ever looked fabulous on Megan's shapeless frame, but she hadn't disputed her sister's statement. There was no changing Ashley's mind once it was made up and if she wanted her to buy this dress, Megan would buy the dress. It was certainly an easier solution than having to pick something out on her own.

She headed through the maze of halls toward the boutique. Thirteen minutes later—three of which were taken up with a phone call from Ashley, who wanted to make sure Megan hadn't forgotten to stop at the mall and then, when she realized her sister was in the boutique, convinced her to let Anne-Marie pick out some jewelry to go with the dress—she was on her way back out again. A relatively quick and painless shopping experience, Megan thought gratefully, as she retraced her steps toward the exit.

An opinion that quickly changed when she stood at the doors and stared out at the rain pounding down on the pavement. With a sigh, she folded the dress bag over her arm and pushed open the door. She was half-way to her car when she realized her keys weren't in her pocket—and totally drenched by the time she turned around again.

She tracked her keys down in Chaundra's Boutique, by the register where she'd set them down to answer her sister's call. She thanked the perpetually smiling Anne-Marie again and left the store, wondering how anyone could be so perky all the time, thanking her lucky stars that she worked in the lab where smiling was optional.

Then she turned the corner and walked into a brick wall.

Okay, so it only felt like a brick wall, Megan acknowledged. What it was, in reality, was a man's chest.

She berated herself for her clumsiness as she lifted her gaze and prepared to apologize. But the words stuck in her throat when she pushed her soggy bangs away from her face and recognized the man standing in front of her.

Gage Richmond.

The younger son of the CEO of Richmond Pharmaceuticals. The man whose mere presence always made her pulse race and her knees quiver.

The first time she'd met him, on her first day of work at the R.P. lab, she'd nearly melted in a puddle at his feet just because he shook her hand. The man was seriously hot—and Megan had been seriously smitten. Not that she would ever admit it, of course. In fact, she went out of her way to avoid him whenever possible because she didn't want him to know that her heart beat a little bit faster whenever he was near. And she didn't want to acknowledge—even to herself—that she was shallow enough to be attracted to a hard body and sexy smile, especially considering her past experience with his type.

On the other hand, no one she'd ever known quite measured up to Gage Richmond. He had thick, light brown hair that curled just above the collar of his shirt, stunning golden brown eyes surrounded by unbelievably long lashes, a strong square jaw and a temptingly shaped mouth. And then there was his body—a long and lean six feet two inches of delicious and delectable male.

"Sorry about that," he said, holding out the keys that had slipped from her grasp when they'd collided.

"My fault," she managed to reply, looking away again and desperately hoping that he wouldn't recognize her.

"No, it was mine. I wasn't paying attention to where I was going." Then he destroyed her meager hope by saying, "It's Megan, right?"

She nodded, a little surprised that he'd remembered. Men like Gage Richmond didn't usually notice women like her, despite the fact that she'd worked for his father's company for almost three years.

"I guess it's really raining out there now," he said.

"I wouldn't know," she said. "I generally just drench myself before coming out in public because I like the wet look."

Ashley had often said her tendency to hide her fears and insecurities behind sarcasm was going to get her in trouble someday and, even as the words spilled out of Megan's mouth, she wished she could yank them back.

But Gage only grinned. "I'd say it's a good look for you except that you're shivering."

"The price women pay to be fashionable."

"How about a cup of coffee to warm you up?"

Gage Richmond was asking *her* to have coffee with *him?* Megan couldn't believe it.

"Or don't you drink coffee?" he prompted.

"No," she said. "I mean, yes. I do drink coffee. But I'm not drinking coffee now. I mean, I don't want any coffee. I want to go home."

Megan could hear the words tumbling out of her mouth, but didn't seem able to stop them. If they'd been in California, she could hope that the ground would open up and swallow her whole. But in Pinehurst, New York, earthquakes were extremely rare, so she was forced to live with the humiliating knowledge that she'd made a complete fool of herself in front of her boss's son.

But Gage either didn't notice or didn't care that she was rambling almost incoherently, because he asked, "Is there anything I can say that would talk you into hanging around for another half an hour or so?"

"Why do you want me to hang around?" she asked bluntly.

He lifted one broad shoulder in a half shrug. "I'm kind of stuck trying to figure out a birthday present and I would really appreciate a woman's input."

"A birthday present?"

"For my seven-year-old niece," he clarified.

"I don't know a lot about kids," she told him.

"Yeah, but you probably know more than me. Please?"

It wasn't the word so much as the silent entreaty in those golden brown eyes. And if there was a woman alive who could say "no" to such a plea—and Gage's reputation led her to believe that there wasn't—she'd have to be a stronger woman than Megan because, even while her mind was scrambling for a reason to refuse, she was nodding her head.

Between his four nieces, Gage had garnered a lot of experience in gift buying over the past several years, most of it successful. But he always seemed to strike out where Lucy was concerned.

His youngest niece was a mystery to him. With the other girls, at least when they were younger, he could usually go into any store and pick up the newest and hottest toy. Of course, Gracie was almost a teenager now, so gift certificates to her favorite clothing stores were an obvious solution. The twins, Eryn and Allie, were close to the double digits and though they had little in common aside from their golden hair and green eyes, were both easily pleased. But Lucy, on the verge of her seventh birthday, continued to baffle him.

She was quiet—which maybe wasn't so unusual considering that she was the youngest of four sisters—and very intense. Whatever she did, she did with 100 percent of her attention on the task, whether that task was reading a book, building a LEGO sculpture or kicking a soccer ball. He'd never known anyone—especially not a child—with such focus.

But the first time he'd met Megan Roarke, he'd been struck by the uncanny sense that he'd just been introduced to the woman his youngest niece would be twenty years in the future. It was more than that they were both blue-eyed blondes—it was the quiet intelligence that shone in their eyes and the concentrated intensity with which they applied themselves to a challenge. So he figured it had to be some kind of sign that he'd arrived at the mall to search for a birthday gift and he'd found the research scientist instead.

He led the way to the toy store and she followed. He knew she wasn't the type to talk unless she had something to say and he didn't mind the silence. It was a pleasant change from frivolous conversation, although he did wonder why she didn't seem to want to talk to and flirt with him, as most women—and particularly those who knew him as the boss's youngest and only unmarried son—were inclined to do.

He pondered this thought as he negotiated through the maze of promotional displays and sale items toward the back section of the store. Then he wondered why he was pondering. So what if Megan wasn't interested in him? He wasn't interested in her, either. She was far too staid, too serious, not at all the type of woman he usually dated.

Of course, he hadn't dated much at all in the past year and he wasn't looking for a date now. He was just looking for help in picking out a birthday gift for his niece.

Megan's eyes widened as she turned down an aisle that was stacked floor to ceiling with pink packages of various shapes and sizes.

"This is where I generally start," he told her. "Usually as long as it's something new and in a big box, Eryn and Allie are happy."

"Then why do you need my help?"

"Because it's Lucy's birthday."

"How many nieces do you have?"

"Four," he answered. "Lucy, who's going to be seven,

is the youngest, the twins—Eryn and Allie—are almost ten and Gracie is twelve."

"I really don't know a lot about kids," Megan said again.

"But you have an advantage over me in that you were once a seven-year-old girl yourself."

"A very long time ago."

He didn't believe it was so very long ago. In fact, considering that she'd completed her master's degree in biochemistry at Columbia University just shortly before she'd started working at Richmond Pharmaceuticals, he would bet she couldn't be more than twenty-eight.

She looked younger, though. Both younger and prettier than he'd expected. Certainly prettier than any woman hiding in a lab should be, even with the thick-framed glasses. She wore little if any makeup, but her features didn't need much artificial enhancement, and the ponytail she habitually wore emphasized the creamy complexion of her skin.

But there was a sweetness about her, too. A gentle innocence that was somehow both intriguing and intimidating. In any event, she was definitely too sweet for a guy like him.

Maybe that was why, prior to their paths crossing unexpectedly tonight, he'd barely given a second thought to Megan Roarke. In fact, he'd never thought about her at all except in relation to her work in the lab.

But their chance meeting—revealing unexpected evidence of her dry sense of humor—had snagged his attention. Or maybe it was the garment bag that had piqued his interest.

His mother bought a lot of her clothes from Chaundra's Boutique, and it surprised him to learn that Megan shopped at the exclusive women's store, too.

She seemed more like the type to buy what she needed from Lab Coats 'R' Us, and it made him wonder exactly what was in the bag draped over her arm.

But he forced his attention away from the woman and to the task at hand.

"Anything bring back fond memories?" he asked, gesturing to the toys that surrounded them.

She paused in front of an elaborate three-story dollhouse, her brow furrowed, as if she was trying to remember. "I didn't play with Barbies. Well, sometimes with my sister," she amended. "But only if I didn't have a choice."

"What did you play with?"

"My all-time favorite gift was a chemistry set—at least until I blew up the kitchen and my mother took it away from me."

"I'll bet that's not a story you told when you interviewed for your job at R.P."

Her lips tilted up at the corners. "Actually, I didn't really blow up the kitchen at all. I just mixed together some ingredients that reacted violently and spewed a sticky mess all over everything."

"Mentos and Coke?" he guessed.

"It was a slight variation on that," she told him, her eyes sparkling behind the lenses of her glasses. "And the explosion much more spectacular."

Gage lost track of what she was saying, stunned by the realization that her eyes weren't blue, as he'd always assumed, but violet.

In the almost three years they'd worked in the same lab—albeit in different areas—he'd never noticed the unique color. On the other hand, there was probably a lot about her that he'd never noticed because she wasn't the type of woman who usually drew his attention. And he was starting to think that might have been a distinct oversight on his part.

"I'm not sure if chemistry is Lucy's thing," he said now, forcing his attention back to the matter at hand. "Although my sister-in-law probably wouldn't appreciate kitchen explosions any less than the bugs her youngest daughter is always bringing into the house."

"She's into bugs?" Megan asked, sounding intrigued.

He nodded. "Completely fascinated by anything creepy-crawly."

"Then that's where you start looking for a gift."

"You're not honestly suggesting that I should give bugs to Lucy?"

"Of course not." She smiled again. "She would probably prefer to get them herself."

Baffled by that response, Gage wordlessly followed Megan to the science & nature department on the other side of the store, where she proceeded to point out magnifying glasses and bug boxes and books and all kinds of other must-haves for an aspiring entomologist.

Gage found her enthusiasm so contagious that there was soon an impressive assortment of packages piled at his feet, beside the dress bag Megan had unceremoniously dumped on top of a display of ladybug houses so that she had both hands free to explore the offerings.

"Look at this," she said, turning to him with yet another box in her hands.

"What is it?"

"It's a NASA-inspired ant farm. The bugs live in and tunnel through the gel, which serves as their food and water, too, so it's very low maintenance. It also has LEDs that highlight the tunnels and let the unit function as a night-light."

"That's…practical," Gage decided. "If maybe a little…weird."

"You don't have to like it," Megan reminded him. "So long as your niece does."

"True," he allowed, even while he wondered if his niece's mother would be so philosophical.

Before Megan could say anything else, her wrist beeped. She glanced at her watch, then thrust the ant farm into his hands. "Sorry," she said. "But I have to run."

"No, I'm sorry for taking up so much of your time," he told her, though he was more sorry that she had to go.

She looked at the pile of potential gifts on the floor, then at the box he held in his hands. "I hope Lucy likes whatever you get for her birthday."

"I'm sure she will, thanks to you."

She smiled at that, then lifted her hand and sort of waved. "I guess I'll see you at work on Monday."

He nodded, and watched as she walked away. Her oversize shirt was tucked into baggy pants that gave no hint of any curves beneath, and yet, the subtle sway of her hips was distinctly feminine and decidedly intriguing.

He shook his head, as if that action might banish the unexpected thought. She really wasn't his type. And even if she was, he had enough on his mind right now without the added complication of a woman.

When she was out of sight, he grabbed a vacant cart and loaded it up—then spotted the abandoned garment bag. Despite his recent admonition, he couldn't deny the anticipation that surged through his veins as he tossed it on top of the pile of gifts.

Now he didn't have to wait until Monday to see the intriguing Megan Roarke again.

Chapter Two

Megan wasn't surprised to find that her sister Ashley's Honda was already in the driveway of the town house they shared when she got home from her trip to the mall. She *was* surprised to see Paige Wilder's Audi parked behind it.

Paige was their cousin, though both Megan and Ashley thought of her as another sister since she'd lived with them while they were in high school, and they always included her in any plans they made together. A family-law attorney with a practice that seemed to get busier and busier each year, Paige had declined more invitations than she'd accepted in recent months, so Megan was doubly pleased that she was there tonight.

As she made her way through the kitchen, following their voices toward the dining room, she noticed the two bottles of merlot on the counter, one of which was already uncorked. Another great thing about Paige—whenever she did make an appearance, she could always be counted on to bring the wine.

"Are we planning on doing some serious drinking tonight?" she asked.

"Is your mother coming?" Paige countered.

Megan had forgotten that detail—or maybe put it deliberately out of her mind.

"In that case, two bottles might not be enough," she warned, accepting the glass that her sister poured for her as she boosted herself onto one of the high-back chairs at the pub-style table.

"I asked Paige to come early so that we could get most of the details worked out before Mom gets here," Ashley explained.

"You mean, before she can take over," Megan said.

Her sister nodded, as Paige muttered, "Good luck with that."

Megan believed that Lillian Roarke had tried to be a good mother to her daughters, and a good aunt to the niece who was dumped in her care whenever a military crisis called Paige's father to duty. The problem was she didn't have a maternal bone in her body.

What Lillian did have were exacting standards and high expectations. And while she appeared outwardly supportive of both of her children, what masqueraded as praise was often barely concealed criticism, and encouragement was often a thinly veiled expression of doubt. Even after twenty-five years, Megan hadn't become immune to her mother's negativity.

Had there not been doctors and nurses present to witness her birth, Megan might have questioned whether there was truly any familial connection between herself and her mother. Lillian had never been the type to wipe tears or kiss boo-boos or snuggle under the covers to chase away bad dreams. But when there were events to be planned—graduations and engagement parties, for example—she was always front and center to ensure that everything was done just right.

Lillian had always been more concerned about appearances than reality, and at the celebration of her daughter's engagement, she would be the smiling and supportive mother-of-the-bride-to-be despite her frequently spoken belief that twenty-eight-year-old Ashley was making a mistake in marrying so quickly—and especially in marrying Trevor Byden.

It was rare for Megan to agree with her mother on anything, but she had to admit—if only to herself—that she shared some of those concerns regarding Ashley's engagement. While she liked Trevor well enough, and there was no doubt that the accountant was devoted to her sister, she wasn't convinced that Ashley loved him as much as she loved what he was offering her—marriage and the hope of having the babies she wanted so badly.

"So where's the dress?" Paige's question jolted her out of her reverie. "I can't wait to see it on you."

"Dress?" Megan echoed, then closed her eyes as realization hit. "Oh, no."

Ashley set a tray of crudités on the table. "Oh, no, *what?*"

Megan swallowed another mouthful of wine. "I kind of—uh—forgot it."

"Forgot it? Where? How?" Her sister impatiently tossed the questions at her. "I talked to you while you were at the boutique buying it."

And Megan knew she'd had the dress when she'd left the store, and when she'd run into Gage and when they'd gone into the toy store. Then she'd put it down some-where and had obviously forgotten to pick it up again. But how could she admit that to her sister?

"I forgot my keys in the boutique," she hedged.

"I'm not worried about your keys," Ashley said.

"And when I went back to get them," she continued as if her sister hadn't spoken, "I ran into someone I know."

"A man," Paige guessed.

Megan frowned. "What makes you think that?"

"There was the slightest hesitation before you said *someone* and your cheeks immediately turned pink."

"You must be deadly on cross-examination," Ashley mused.

"It's a talent," Paige acknowledged, then turned her attention back to Megan. "So—who is he?"

"Just someone from the lab."

"Workplace romances are inherently plagued with problems," her cousin warned.

"There's no romance."

"Obviously *something* happened to make you forget your dress," Ashley pointed out.

"He asked me to help him pick out a birthday gift."

"Not for another woman?" Paige demanded.

Megan shook her head. "For his niece."

"Oh." Her sister smiled. "That's sweet."

It *was* kind of sweet. And after Megan had gotten over the nervousness evoked by Gage's mere presence, she'd been impressed to realize that he really did care about finding a gift the little girl would like.

"So we went to the toy store, and I must have put the dress down—"

"And picked up stars in your eyes," Paige interjected.

Megan shook her head. "I have no illusions."

Ashley frowned. "What is that supposed to mean?"

"He's just not the type of man who would ever notice a woman like me."

"Define *a woman like you*," Paige demanded.

Megan loved that her cousin and her sister were so quick to defend her, but family loyalty didn't allow either of them to see her as clearly as she saw herself. She wasn't beautiful or sexy or charismatic, qualities that both Paige and Ashley had in spades. She was the girl next door, the reliable friend, the neighborhood pal. And that was why she and Gage Richmond would never be anything more than colleagues and possibly friends.

"I only meant—"

The doorbell chimed, sounding a reprieve.

"That will be Mom," she said, pushing her chair away from the table.

"Mom doesn't ring the doorbell," Ashley reminded her.

When Megan opened the door, her sister's statement was confirmed. It wasn't Lillian Roarke on the doorstep. It was Gage Richmond.

"I called Lois Edmond in H.R. to find out where you lived," he told her.

"Why?" Megan asked, too stunned by his unexpected appearance to think of anything else to say.

"Because you forgot this—" he held up the bag from Chaundra's Boutique "—in the toy store, and I didn't know if it was something you needed tonight."

She shook her head. "No, it's not. But thank you."

"You're welcome."

Before Megan could say anything else, she heard footsteps in the hall and knew that curiosity had drawn her sister and her cousin to the door to check out their visitor.

"Hi, I'm Ashley," she said. "Megan's sister."

"I would have guessed that," he said.

"Really?" Ashley said, while Megan resisted the urge

to snort her disbelief. No one who didn't already know they were related had ever commented on a resemblance between the sisters.

"You have the same eyes," he explained, an observation that made Megan rethink her own opinion of Gage Richmond.

While people frequently commented on Ashley's unusual eyes, they rarely took note of Megan's, hidden behind her glasses. Maybe he wasn't quite as shallow and self-absorbed as he was painted by his reputation.

"Handsome *and* observant," Paige noted with approval.

Megan found herself wishing for an earthquake again. Hadn't she embarrassed herself in front of the boss's son enough already without her sister and cousin adding to her humiliation?

"My cousin Paige," Megan told him, reluctantly making the introduction.

"And you are?" Ashley prompted the man on the doorstep.

"Would you believe the deliveryman from the boutique?" Megan suggested before Gage could reply.

"No," her sister replied flatly, not taking her eyes off of Gage.

Not that Megan could blame her for that.

"Gage Richmond," he said, and offered one of his infamous heart-stopping smiles.

"Thanks for bringing the bag," Megan said, silently urging him along before her well-intentioned but misguided family members could say or do anything to embarrass her further. After all, she didn't need their help when she'd already done a fine job of that entirely on her own.

"Yes, thank you," Ashley said. "Since the dress is for

my engagement party, I very much appreciate that you returned it to Megan."

"It was my pleasure," Gage said. "And bringing it by gave me another chance to thank your sister for her help with my shopping."

"Handsome, observant, considerate and apprecia-tive," Paige amended, with a nod of approval. "Why don't you come in for a glass of wine so we can chat some more?"

"I'm sure Gage has somewhere else that he needs to be," Megan interrupted quickly, desperately.

She caught the gleam of amusement in his eyes and sus-pected that he was considering Paige's invitation, if only because he knew she didn't want him to. But when he finally spoke, it was to say, "As a matter of fact, I should be getting home. I have some birthday presents to wrap."

"Another time?" Paige said.

"Thank you again." Megan spoke clearly, deter-mined to take control of the situation—and the flutters in her tummy.

Gage nodded, accepting the dismissal, before turning his attention to the two women hovering in the doorway behind her. "It was nice meeting you both."

"You, too," they chorused, leaning closer to watch him walk down the driveway.

Though Megan was probably even more reluctant to tear her gaze from his retreating form, she firmly closed the door and turned back toward the kitchen.

Paige raised her brows. "Now I understand why you forgot the dress."

Megan held the bag aloft, eager to talk about any-thing but Gage Richmond. "Didn't you say you wanted to see this?"

"Later." Ashley took it from her and hung it in the

closet. "Right now, I want to hear more about Mr. Tall, Dark and Yummy."

"There's nothing more to tell," Megan insisted, turning back toward the kitchen as the door opened behind her again.

As Ashley had noted when the bell rang earlier, their mother wasn't the type to observe such formalities at their home.

"Who was that just leaving?" Lillian Roarke asked in lieu of a greeting.

Before Megan could reply, Paige said, "That was Megan's new boyfriend."

Gage was wrapping Lucy's presents—or at least stuffing them into decorative bags with tissue—when Allan Richmond stopped by on his way home after a late meeting. He'd seen his dad at work earlier and would be seeing him again at Lucy's birthday party the next day, so Gage guessed there was a specific reason for this visit now, even if he couldn't figure out what that might be.

He offered his father a beer and a microwaved meal. Allan took the drink but declined the frozen lasagna.

"Grace is holding dinner for me," he explained.

"Must be nice to go home to a hot meal," Gage said, shoving the box back into the freezer.

"It's even nicer to have someone to go home to."

"Is that the real reason you stopped by—to extol the virtues of married life?"

It certainly wouldn't be the first time—nor the last. Though Gage couldn't remember exactly when his parents had become so interested in his marital status, he thought it was some time after his brother and sister-in-law had announced—after the birth of their fourth child—that they weren't planning on having any more.

Grace absolutely doted on her grandbabies and had apparently turned her attention to her younger son in the hope that he would settle down and add to the clan.

Actually, Craig and Gage were Grace's stepsons, but she had always been more of a mother to the boys than the woman who had given birth to them. As a result, there wasn't anything Gage wouldn't do for Grace—except marry and have children.

"No," his father responded to his question. "I stopped by to tell you that Dean Garrison is planning to retire at the end of the summer."

The announcement wasn't really news to Gage. Garrison, the current vice president of Clinical Science, had been talking about retirement for a few years now.

"You're one of several candidates whose name has been put forward to fill the position."

"One of several?" Gage echoed, unable to hide his surprise.

Though no explicit promises had ever been made, he'd always believed that the job would be his when Garrison retired. It was all he'd ever wanted, everything he'd worked toward.

"I want to give you the job," Allan told him.

"But?"

"But the fact that your name is Richmond isn't justification enough. You need to prove that you're V.P. material."

"Hasn't my work over the past half dozen years proven it already?"

"Your work has been exemplary. It's your reputation outside of work that has led some of our more conservative board members to question your maturity and commitment."

"My reputation outside of work?" he found himself echoing his father's words again.

"Your inability to commit to a relationship," Allan clarified. "Moving from one relationship to another, from one woman to another, could give the impression that you're shortsighted—unable or unwilling to focus on the long-term.

"Face it, Gage. You've earned yourself quite the reputation as a playboy and that's not the image we want for our executives at Richmond Pharmaceuticals. Until you settle down, I can't—and I won't—go to bat for you with the board."

"I used to date a lot of different women," he acknowledged. "But I haven't been dating at all in the past few months."

"Why is that?"

He shrugged. "I've been busy."

His father finished his beer and set the empty bottle down. "Maybe that's true."

"What else could it be?"

"Do you really want to know what I think?"

Gage wasn't sure, but he nodded anyway.

"I think—I *hope*—you might finally have realized that you've been wasting your time with women who are completely wrong for you."

"That's assuming there's a woman out there somewhere who's right for me."

"There is," Allan said with certainty. "And when you find her, you'll know it."

Gage wasn't convinced. He also wasn't looking for any "right" woman. He liked being able to come and go as he pleased, not being accountable to anyone but himself. He was happy with his life—or he would be, as soon as he was in the V.P. office.

And now he had a specific timeline to focus his efforts: six months. He'd been given half a year to prove to his father and the rest of the board of directors at Richmond Pharmaceuticals that he was mature and responsible—like his brother, Craig.

Allan Richmond might not have mentioned his older son's name out loud, but the comparison was implied. Gage had always been measured against his brother, and he'd always come up short. The fact that Craig was already a V.P. and Gage was not was proof of that.

But what else did Craig have that Gage didn't?

A wife and four kids.

He frowned at the answer that immediately sprang to mind, because he had no intention of following his brother's footsteps down the matrimonial path. He didn't want to get married. He didn't want to settle down. Maybe a wife and family was the American dream for a lot of men, but to him, it was a nightmare.

As a child caught in the middle of a nasty custody battle between his parents, he'd learned early on to protect himself. He put up safeguards around his heart so that every time he moved from his father's house to his mother's and back again, it hurt a little less. When his mother left for the last time, he almost didn't care.

And he hadn't let himself love another woman since. Not the head-over-heels type of love, anyway. Maybe he'd come close a couple of times, but he'd always pulled back before he got in too deep. Even with Beth, his only serious long-term girlfriend and the only woman he'd even believed himself to be in love with, he'd been the one to leave rather than be left behind.

And thankfully he'd been mistaken about the whole love thing, which he proved by putting Beth out of his mind and concentrating on his career. And any woman who claimed he didn't know the meaning of commitment didn't understand him at all, because he was already committed to his job. And now he had a new focus—to ensure that the V.P. office would be his by the end of the summer.

It was almost ten o'clock before Lillian Roarke was finally satisfied that all the necessary details for the engagement party had been taken care of and said good-night to her daughters and niece. Ashley went to her room to call her fiancé and update him on the plans, and Megan turned to Paige and demanded, "What have you done?"

Her cousin didn't feign ignorance or apology. "I got your mother off your back for one night," she said.

"But now she thinks I have a boyfriend, which she interpreted to mean a date for Ashley's engagement party."

"And you will have, as soon as you invite Gage Richmond to go with you."

Megan shook her head. "I barely know the man."

"You know him well enough to help him shop for a birthday gift for his niece."

"We happened to cross paths at the mall and he was desperate."

"Well, happen to cross paths with him at work and tell him that *you're* desperate."

"Yeah, I can see how that kind of approach would appeal," she said drily.

Paige laughed as she sorted the lists and notes that littered the table. "I'll bet it's one he hasn't heard before."

"And not one he's going to hear from me," Megan said.

"Why not? What are you afraid of?"

"I'm not afraid," she denied. "But you know I don't have the best track record with men."

"You've made a few errors in judgment," Paige acknowledged with a shrug. "So have I. So has your sister."

Megan guessed her cousin's thoughts were on a similar path to her own—wondering if Trevor Byden was Ashley's prince charming or another error in judgment. She pushed the thought aside and picked up her wineglass.

"Asking Gage Richmond out on a date wouldn't be an error in judgment," she finally said. "It would be an invitation to humiliation."

"Why do you say that?"

"Because the man is a major leaguer when it comes to dating and I'm still at the T-ball stage."

Paige smiled at the analogy. "Well, that major leaguer seemed majorly interested in playing ball with you."

"Because he delivered a dress that I was careless enough to leave in a toy store?" she asked skeptically.

"Because he couldn't take his eyes off of you the whole time he was here."

Megan shook her head. She wished it was true but experience had proven that men like Gage Richmond were oblivious to her.

"And no one else will be able to take their eyes off of you when you walk into your sister's engagement party with him."

Except that Megan would walk into the party alone, and her mother would pretend to hide her disappointment.

As a child, her relatives had often referred to her as "poor little Megan" because she was too shy to make friends, preferring to hide in a corner rather than make conversation with people she didn't know. She might not be "little" anymore, but nothing else had changed.

"I can picture it clearly," Paige continued. "The surprise and envy on everyone's faces—most notably our cousin Camilla's—when you show up with that sexy man at your side."

Showing up with Gage would definitely create some

ripples in the family pond, especially by the ruffled feathers of those who had grown so smug about Megan's solo appearance at social events.

"Forget it," she said. "I'll think about inviting a date to the party, but it won't be Gage Richmond."

Paige's lips curved as she tipped the last of the wine into her cousin's glass. "I dare you."

Megan narrowed her eyes. "I'm not ten years old anymore. You can't get me to do something I don't want to simply by uttering those three words."

"How about bribery?"

She sipped her wine.

"Of course, not having to listen to your mother's commentary about the importance of putting on some lipstick if you ever want to meet a nice man should be incentive enough," Paige told her, "but I'll sweeten the deal.

"If you invite Gage Richmond to be your date for Ashley's engagement party, we'll all go to Gia's Spa before the event. My treat."

Megan had never cared much about the latest hairstyles or makeup trends, but she did enjoy a good foot treatment, and Gia's were absolutely the best. "Do I get the pedicure even if he says no?"

"I'll only know for sure that you asked if he says yes," her cousin pointed out.

She frowned at that. "He won't say yes."

"Ask him." Paige tossed back the last of her wine then grinned wickedly. "And maybe the next time he gives you back your clothes, it will be after he picks them up off the floor beside his bed."

Chapter Three

Bugs, Gage mused, as he made his way toward the employee café to grab a cup of coffee on the Monday morning after Lucy's birthday party. Who would have guessed that a seven-year-old girl would get so excited about bugs?

He certainly wouldn't, which was why he'd been so far off base with the other gifts he'd given to Lucy over the years. He'd assumed—obviously incorrectly—that just because she was a girl, she'd like baby dolls and ballet slippers. And he would have struck out again if he hadn't dragged Megan Roarke into the toy store with him.

Thinking of Megan now, he realized he might have made some incorrect assumptions where she was concerned, too. There was a lot more to her than he'd originally suspected.

He spotted her at the counter as soon as he entered the café, as if she'd been conjured by his thoughts. She

was alone, as she frequently was, and apparently preoccupied by her own thoughts as she added milk and
sugar to her coffee.

He smiled, genuinely pleased to see her and eager to
tell her about the success of his shopping expedition.
But he hesitated, his recent conversation with his father
still lingering in the back of his mind.

In his younger days, he had sometimes been less than
discreet while dating an employee of R.P.—and he'd dated
quite a few women from the company. Of course, none of
those relationships had been serious or long-term, and it
hadn't been long before coworkers started placing bets on
the duration of a new romance. Gage hadn't learned about
this pool until it had been going on for a while, and when
he did, he vowed to stop dating women from work.

That was a few years ago now, but he still worried
that seeking out Megan in a public venue might start the
rumor mill churning again. On the other hand, he was
confident that people would know his relationship with
the researcher was strictly professional. After all, she
wasn't at all like the type of woman he usually dated.

*You've been wasting your time with women who are
completely wrong for you.*

Maybe that was true, but he had no intention of looking for a different type of woman in the hope of meeting
someone who was right for him, especially when he still
didn't believe he would—and didn't want to—find one
who was.

Anyway, there was no point in tempting fate—or gossip. Although he'd like to tell Megan about the birthday
party, it was probably better if he simply took his coffee
back to the office, as if he'd never seen her there.

Except that she looked up then, their eyes met across
the room…and *she* looked away.

As if she didn't even know him.

Or maybe as if she didn't expect him to acknowledge that he knew her.

The thought niggled at his conscience, and he found himself carrying his cup toward the table at which she'd sat down.

"Do you mind if I join you?" he asked, indicating the empty chair across from her.

"Um, sure. I mean, no, I don't mind." She dropped her gaze and lifted her cup to her mouth.

Gage sat down. "I'm Lucy's favorite uncle this week."

She looked up at that. "Your birthday gift was a hit?"

"My niece was over the moon with everything and anxious to put all of her new tools and toys to use."

"All of?" she prompted.

He shrugged. "I had trouble narrowing down my selections, so I just bought everything you picked out."

She smiled. "No wonder she was happy."

"Her enthusiasm was dampened only slightly by her mother's request that she wait for the backyard to dry out a little before she tramped through the muck, looking for specimens."

"I guess you forgot the rubber boots."

"I guess I did," he agreed.

She smiled again, and he found his gaze shifting to her mouth.

She wore no color or gloss, but her lips—naturally pink and full—were somehow even more tempting without any enhancement.

Tempting? He gave himself a mental shake. Okay, so he'd realized he'd made some inaccurate assumptions about Megan, but he wasn't—couldn't possibly be—attracted to her.

Still, he couldn't help but notice her great bone structure and creamy, flawless skin. Or that her hair wasn't just blond but shot through with strands of flaxen and gold that glinted in the light. True, she had more angles than curves and he generally liked his women on the softer side, but she still had the most intriguing violet eyes he'd ever seen.

"Anyway," he said, forcing his attention back to the topic at hand. "I owe you. And if there's ever anything I can do for you—any way I could possibly repay you—you only have to ask."

"It wasn't a big deal. Really."

"It *was* a really big deal," he argued.

"I was glad to help." She glanced at her watch. "But now I need to be getting back to work."

"You're entitled to a half-hour break and you haven't been here half of that."

"I want to finish a report I'm writing."

"Is that the final report on Fedentropin?" he asked, referring to the drug she had helped develop for women suffering from endometriosis.

"How did you know?"

"I was talking to Dean Garrison this morning about possible timelines for the upcoming trial."

Megan sat back down. "Is it going to start soon, then?"

"Within the next couple of months."

"That's great."

"Garrison said you've been putting a lot of extra hours into the project."

"It means a lot to me," she admitted.

"Then you'll be pleased to know that he wants you and me to coordinate the trial."

"He told me he was going to make a recommendation," she confessed, her voice tinged with both hope and excitement. "I didn't know it was actually going to happen."

Gage had been less than thrilled by the news himself.

Not that he had any objection to working with Megan. But he'd thought running the trial would have been a good opportunity to prove himself, to demonstrate that he had the requisite skills and experience to fill the V.P. position.

Learning that he would have to share the responsibilities was a disappointment, but maybe sharing it with Megan wouldn't be so bad. And it would give him the perfect opportunity to get to know her better.

There were three messages on Megan's answering machine when she got home Monday night. A quick glance at the call display confirmed that they were all from Paige. She punched the erase button without listening to them. No doubt they all said exactly the same thing as the e-mails she'd sent to Megan's computer at work and the text messages to her cell phone.

Have you asked him yet?

She wasn't ready to call her back. She didn't want to admit to her cousin that she hadn't—and wouldn't—invite Gage to Ashley's engagement party. Because as many reasons as she had for wanting to ask him to be her date, there were a lot more reasons *not* to ask. Most notably, her conviction that he would say no. Because once the question had been asked, it couldn't be unasked. There could be no taking back the words or the embarrassment and humiliation she would inevitably feel when he declined the invitation.

And if there's ever anything I can do for you, any way I could possibly repay you, you only have to ask.

Megan ignored the echo of Gage's words in the back of her mind as she made her way into the kitchen to scrounge up something for dinner.

She was certain he hadn't really meant them. It was just the kind of thing someone said to express appreciation. And if she did ask him for a favor in return—especially something so personal as to be her date for her sister's engagement party—it would put both of them in an awkward position. Gage while he scrambled to come up with a plausible excuse for refusing, and Megan while she tried to pretend his response didn't really matter.

Ashley came down the stairs, clothes neatly pressed, makeup freshly reapplied. Despite her outwardly casual appearance, Megan could see the tension in her eyes.

"Parent-teacher conferences tonight," she suddenly remembered.

Her sister nodded. "I love the kids—it's the parents I sometimes wish I could sit in the corners for a time-out."

"They'll love you," she assured her, kissing Ashley's cheek. "They always do."

"Not always. But thanks for the vote of confidence." She swung her tote bag over her shoulder. "By the way, Paige has been trying to get in touch with you."

"Yeah, I got a dozen or so messages along that line."

"She wanted to let you know that she's booked pedicures for two o'clock on Saturday."

"She always did fight dirty," Megan grumbled.

"As only someone who truly knows and loves you can do."

"I won't be bribed or blackmailed," she said decisively. "I'll call Gia and make my own appointment."

"Good luck. Apparently Paige booked the entire spa for the whole afternoon. If you want an appointment, you'll have to get a date."

"I hate her."

Ashley laughed as she made her way to the door.

"She outmaneuvered you on this one but, if you stopped being mad at her for two minutes, you might realize this is a win-win situation."

Or Megan could lose the bet, her pride and her heart. And that was a risk she had vowed never to take again.

Gage went for lunch with his dad and his brother on Thursday, as they tried to do at least once a month. Sometimes they chatted about business, sometimes about nothing in particular, but always it was a time the three men enjoyed together.

"I'm glad to see you're taking my advice," Allan said, as he stirred cream into his coffee.

"About?"

"Finding a nice young woman. A different kind of woman."

Gage frowned, wondering what his father was talking about. Only a few days had passed since he'd learned about Garrison's retirement and his father's conviction that he could prove his maturity by settling down, and he hadn't been out with anyone since then. In fact, aside from having coffee with Megan…

He glanced at his brother, who lifted his shoulder in silent apology. "I happened to mention that I saw you and Megan Roarke in the cafeteria the other day."

"A lovely girl," Allan interjected. "Not your usual type, which is why I was so surprised when Craig told me."

Told him *what?* Gage wondered, starting to feel more than a little bit uncomfortable with the implications of his father's words. He looked to his brother for help, but Craig was focused on his cheesecake—or maybe just focused on avoiding Gage's silent plea for help.

"And I'll admit to some initial concern about your

working relationship," Allan continued. "But the more I thought about it, the more I realized she's exactly the type of woman you need—"

His father thought Megan was the type of woman he needed? Gage wasn't just uncomfortable now, he was completely baffled. Where would he ever get such an idea? How had his usually rational father made the hugely irrational leap from a cafeteria meeting to a personal relationship?

"—and I trust that you will both continue to behave professionally in the lab."

There were so many assumptions in his statement that Gage wasn't sure where to begin to refute them, so he only said, "I think you're reading too much into a cup of coffee."

"Am I?" Allan sounded disappointed.

Again, Gage looked at Craig, but his brother remained intent on finishing his dessert, leaving him to fend for himself. Or maybe Craig also believed that Gage was involved with Megan.

Gage frowned over this thought as he considered his response to his father's question. The last thing he wanted was to have yet another dialogue with his father about his dating habits, but he had to correct his mistaken assumption about his relationship with Megan.

Or did he?

He mulled over that question as he sipped his own coffee.

Maybe if his dad believed Gage was seeing Megan, a woman he obviously approved of, Allan would be more willing to support him in his bid for the V.P. position. And it wasn't entirely untrue, since they would be seeing a lot of one another while they were working on the Fedentropin trial together.

"It's just that it's kind of, uh, premature to talk about where things might go with Megan and I," Gage said.

His father nodded. "The beginning of a new relationship can be difficult enough without the pressure of any extra scrutiny."

Gage didn't quite meet his gaze. "Thanks for understanding."

"But I know your mother would love to meet her, whenever you're ready," Allan continued.

Craig pushed his now-empty plate aside.

"I'll let you know," Gage told his father, even as he wondered, *What have I gotten myself into now?*

By Thursday afternoon, two days before Ashley's engagement party, Paige still hadn't let up in her campaign to convince Megan to invite Gage to the big event. By then, Megan was sure she'd waited too long. There was no way he didn't already have plans for Saturday night. Men like Gage Richmond always had Saturday-night plans.

So when he returned to the lab after his lunch, she decided to broach the subject in the hope that finally doing so might convince Paige to let her have the spa appointment she'd made.

He glanced up when she approached his desk, and she saw surprise—then something else that she thought might have been pleasure—flicker in his eyes. Then he smiled, and her heart leaped and her knees quivered, and she knew this was a bad idea. Definitely a very bad idea.

"Hi, Megan."

As much as she was tempted to turn around and walk away, she knew she had to see this through. She forced a smile, considered her words. She'd never been very good with chit-chat and was too nervous to waste time on idle chatter anyway, so she simply blurted out, "Do you remember saying that if I ever needed a favor, I could come to you?"

"Sure," Gage agreed easily.

"Well, I need a favor."

He smiled. "I got that part. What do you need?"

She drew a deep breath. "A date."

He raised his eyebrows. "For what? When?"

"My sister's engagement party. Saturday night."

He didn't blink at the mention of an engagement party, the type of occasion that would make most men—especially those of only casual acquaintance—balk. All he said was, "*This* Saturday?"

She nodded. "I know it's short notice and I'm sure you already have plans but—"

"What time should I pick you up?" he interrupted.

She stared at him. Blinked.

He waited patiently, that sexy half smile on his face, while she scrambled to unscramble her brain and find her voice again.

"You want to go…with me?"

"Sure," he said again.

She opened her mouth, then snapped it shut.

If he was willing to be her date for Saturday night, who was she to try to talk him out of it?

"Time?" he prompted.

"Eight o'clock. At the country club. But I should probably be there a little earlier than that."

"I'll pick you up at seven."

"Great. That would be—um—great." She was still a little baffled by his easy acceptance. "Thanks."

She turned around and went back to her own work station, not entirely sure she comprehended what had just happened.

Apparently she had a date with Gage Richmond. She'd asked—and he'd said yes without any hesitation. In fact, he'd seemed almost eager to accept her invitation.

But why?

A woman with a genius IQ was smart enough to know that a man who hadn't looked twice in her direction in the three years she'd worked at Richmond Pharmaceuticals wasn't suddenly overwhelmed by the desire to spend time in her company. No, she was certain that Gage Richmond had an agenda. Men like him always did.

And despite the rather sheltered life she'd led, she had known men like him before. Men who were far too good-looking, too charming and too self-confident for a woman like her to stand a chance.

She'd been taken in by seductive eyes and sexy smiles before and wouldn't fall easily again. Of course, the first time had been when she was only in high school and assigned as a lab partner to the captain of the football team. On the first day of class, Darrin Walsh had given her a slow, bone-melting smile that had made her his willing slave—then he went on to flirt with the cheerleaders while she wrote up his reports.

She'd learned her lesson from that—or so she'd thought until she'd fallen head over heels in college. Sam Meyer had been another teaching assistant in the biochemistry department, and the first man she'd really thought understood her hopes and dreams—until he stole one of her research papers and tried to pass it off as his own. He'd been expelled and she'd vowed never to trust her fickle heart again.

Then came Bill Penske. He'd been more her type— a little shy, a little geeky, a lot inexperienced. He'd been her first lover, and she'd been his. The event had been so uninspiring that Megan hadn't found herself wanting to do it again. They'd parted ways only a few weeks later.

She was older now, and wiser, and though she'd dated casually and infrequently since then, she knew that she was still completely out of her league with a man like Gage Richmond.

But whatever his agenda, she could hardly object when she had one of her own.

She only hoped she wouldn't regret it.

Chapter Four

I have a date.

It was the first thought on Megan's mind when she woke up Saturday morning, and one that immediately caused a full-scale panic.

Because she didn't just have a date—she had a date with Gage Richmond. Her boss's son. Heir to a pharmaceutical empire. And the most spectacular-looking man she'd ever met.

Megan groaned aloud as the full impact of what she'd done finally hit her. Who did she think she was kidding? Anyone who saw the two of them together would know that Gage was doing her a favor.

"Rise and shine, sleepyhead." Ashley pushed open the curtains so that sunlight spilled through the window. "We've got things to do today."

Megan pulled the covers up over her head. "I changed my mind."

"You can't change your mind."

"I'm sick."

Ashley yanked back the covers and touched the back of her hand to her sister's forehead. "Lying fibberitis?" she guessed.

Megan stuck her tongue out at her.

"Immature lying fibberitis," Ashley amended her diagnosis.

"I feel clammy and weak. My stomach is in knots and my heart is pounding."

"Those are signs of anticipation, not a viral infection."

"Remember you said that when I throw up on you."

"You're not going to throw up."

"I really don't want to do this."

"I really don't care," Ashley said unsympathetically, tossing a pair of jeans and a blouse onto her sister's bed. "Get dressed—we're meeting Paige for brunch and some shopping before our appointment at Gia's."

"I don't want to go for brunch. I hate shopping. And I love you, Ashley, but I really don't want to go to your engagement party."

"You want to go," Ashley insisted. "You want everyone who ever dared pity you for being alone to see you with Gage, but you're afraid that he won't show up so you're pretending to be sick so that you can cancel before he has a chance to stand you up."

It was such an accurate assessment of everything she was feeling that Megan could only stare. "How do you know these things?"

"Because I'm your sister and, believe it or not, everything that you're feeling is completely normal."

"Maybe he won't show."

"He'll be here."

"How do you know?"

"He's a good guy. Thoughtful. Solid. Dependable."

"You got all of that from a five-minute conversation on the doorstep?"

"An initial impression that was reinforced by our telephone conversation this morning."

"He called you?"

"I think he was actually calling *you*," Ashley explained. "But when I told him you were still sleeping, he settled for talking to me."

"Was he calling to cancel?"

"No, he was calling to see if the party was black tie."

"Is it?"

Ashley smiled. "No. But I was impressed that he would think to ask, that it would matter to him to be appropriately dressed for his first date with you."

"First and last," Megan mumbled.

"Give him a chance."

"Come on, Ash. You know it's not him, it's me. I get nervous and I don't know what to say. Or, worse, I start talking about work, because it's the only thing I'm comfortable talking about. After a half an hour in my company, he'll be looking for excuses to head for the door."

"Just give him a chance," her sister said again.

She sighed. She could give him a chance, but she could not—would not—give him her heart.

Megan, Ashley and Paige had certain traditions. Every month they met on the first Friday for a girls' night and on the third Sunday for brunch. Saturday gettogethers were less structured and less frequent, but Ashley had a complete agenda for the day of her engagement party.

The morning started with breakfast at Michelynne's, a little café tucked amidst the trendy bistros and exclusive boutiques of the village—which would be their after-breakfast shopping destination.

If Megan's retail anxiety and fear of crowds combined to make her hyperventilate in the parking lot of the mall, as had occasionally happened, she was ten times more apprehensive about "Shopping on Rockton" as the banners attached to the decorative streetlamps encouraged passersby to do. So there was absolutely no way she was venturing into that labyrinth filled with anorexic salesgirls, whose glossy smiles were as fake as their silicone breasts—at least not on an empty stomach.

Paige had already secured a table and was sipping an oversize cup of café au lait when Megan and Ashley arrived.

The hostess, who escorted them to their table and handed out the menus, asked if they wanted coffee. Before Megan could respond in the affirmative, Ashley shook her head and said, "Mimosas all around."

Megan arched a brow but made no protest. If she was going to get through this day, including shopping, the spa and her date with Gage, a little bit of alcohol might be just what she needed to blunt the edge of her ever-increasing anxiety.

"Since we're having champagne—in celebration of the occasion of your engagement party, I presume," Paige said to Ashley, raising her glass, "I would like to propose a toast to the bride-to-be and to happy endings."

"And to happy beginnings," Ashley added, with a pointed look in her sister's direction.

Megan tapped her glass to the others.

"And to getting through the next twelve hours without throwing up," she added.

Paige laughed; Ashley just shook her head.

While they sipped their mimosas and ate Belgian

waffles piled high with fresh fruit and mounds of whipped cream, they chatted about inconsequential topics. Or maybe it was only Megan who thought the topics were inconsequential, as Paige seemed to carefully consider everything Ashley said about her search for the perfect bridesmaid dresses while she tried not to think about her upcoming date with Gage Richmond.

Gage had a date.

While that fact in and of itself wasn't unusual, he was having second thoughts about this one. Or maybe it would be more accurate to say he was having second thoughts about his reasons for accompanying Megan to her sister's engagement party.

He liked his colleague well enough, and he certainly admired her intelligence, but he wasn't sure why he'd agreed to be her date for the evening. He wanted to believe it was simply because she'd asked, or maybe because he really did owe her a favor for helping him shop for Lucy's birthday gift.

But if he was honest with himself, as he usually tried to be, he would admit that his willing acceptance of her invitation had been—at least partly—motivated by a desire to perpetuate his father's mistaken belief that he was dating Megan. And since tonight *was* a date, that belief would no longer be mistaken.

Except that, from Megan's perspective, it wasn't a date but a favor.

He was frowning over that when the phone rang.

The frown immediately turned into a smile when he heard Grace Richmond's voice on the line.

Since his biological mother had walked out on her husband and kids when Gage was still a baby, and disappeared from his life entirely only a few years later, Grace was the only mother he'd ever really known. His earliest memories were of Grace, her gentle smile and warm hugs.

It was Grace who had read him bedtime stories, who had taken him to his first day of kindergarten, and who had sat in the emergency room with him when he'd needed seven stitches to close the gash in his knee after he'd slipped on a pile of rocks that she'd warned him against climbing on in the first place and never said "I told you so".

She was the one woman—the only woman—he'd always been able to count on. The only woman he'd ever really loved.

He thought fleetingly of Beth, and of feelings that had been just as transitory. The lessons he'd learned from that relationship, however, had not been easily forgotten.

"Craig and Tess and the kids are coming over for dinner tonight," Grace told him. "And I thought you might like to join us."

"You know I'd never turn down a free meal," Gage said. "Unless I had other plans."

"You're saying you do?" she guessed.

"A date," he confirmed, wondering again why this date seemed different from so many others, and why he felt such a strong pull toward Megan when she was so different from any other woman he'd ever dated.

Grace paused a moment, then asked, "With the flight attendant?"

"Flight attendant? Oh, Carol-Ann," he remembered, thinking back. "No. I haven't seen her in at least five months."

Though she didn't say so, he knew she wasn't disappointed by the news. Grace had met Carol-Ann only once, at a fundraising event for the new Pinehurst Library, and had never—until now—asked about her again.

"You're seeing someone new?" she prompted.

"I'm not sure this one date will lead to anything more than that," he said, still uncertain as to whether he hoped it would or wouldn't.

For her part, Megan didn't seem to have any expectations about the evening ahead. In fact, when she'd invited him to the party, he'd got the impression that she expected him to refuse. Maybe she'd even *wanted* him to refuse. But if that was the case, why had she even invited him?

"Is she a vegetarian?" Grace's question interrupted his speculation.

"I have no idea."

"Because if she's not, your father's grilling steaks tonight if you wanted to bring her by—"

"—so that you can grill her?" Gage guessed.

"So that your dad and I can *meet* her," she chided.

Though he knew it was dangerous to give his mother too much information, he couldn't resist baiting her, just a little. "Dad's already met her," he said. "In fact, he's known her longer than I have."

"Then it's someone from work."

"You can think whatever you want," Gage said, unable to deny it.

"Megan Roarke," she guessed.

He scowled. "How did you come up with that name?"

"Your dad told me about her. He said you were going to be working on a big project together, but he didn't mention that you were dating her."

Gage knew that if she could see him, she would undoubtedly see that he was squirming inside because that one little white lie had taken on a life of its own. Or maybe because a brief flash of attraction seemed to be growing into something more.

"Don't go reading too much into anything," he said. "It's just one date."

"What are your plans for this date?"

"We're going to a party," he admitted.

"A party?"

He gave in, because he knew she wouldn't give up and he simply couldn't lie to her. "It's Megan's sister's engagement party."

"Oh. Well." He could hear the smile in her voice. "That's quite a first date."

"Don't."

"Don't what?" she asked innocently.

"Read anything into it."

"I wouldn't dream of it," she said, though the amusement in her tone belied the words. "But I should let you go. I wouldn't want you to be late for your engagement party."

"It's not *my* engagement party."

"I'll give you a call tomorrow."

Gage wondered if her words were a promise or a threat.

More, he wondered why he'd told her as much as he had.

Had he wanted her to know about his date with Megan, so that she could pass on the information to his father, further promoting the idea that he was in a relationship with this woman? Or because he was actually interested in Megan and suspected that his mother would be meeting her sometime soon?

Because he didn't know the answers to these questions, he pushed them aside to get ready for his date.

As the minutes ticked closer and closer to seven o'clock, Megan grew more and more certain that the night was going to be a disaster.

"Relax. It's not going to be a disaster," Paige said.

Megan frowned. "Did I say that out loud?"

Her cousin laughed. "No, but I know the way your mind works—and despite the exquisite job Gia did with your makeup, your face is pale and you're clenching your jaw."

"What if he doesn't show up?"

"He'll be here."

"How do you know?"

"Because he's not Darrin."

"Thanks for that reminder," she muttered sarcastically.

"As if your mind wasn't already spinning in that direction."

Megan refused to acknowledge that fact, because doing so would be to admit that she'd never fully gotten over the humiliation of being invited to the prom by a guy who never showed up.

"Gage will be here," Paige said again. "Which means that we need to get you into your dress."

"That's why you're really here, isn't it? Because Ashley's afraid that I might duck and run."

"Your sister knows you would never let her down," her cousin said, the pointed tone bringing a guilty flush to Megan's cheeks. "And I know that everyone gets a little nervous before a first date sometimes."

"Speaking of dates." Megan opened the closet to reach for her dress. "Is Josh picking you up here?"

Paige shook her head. "No, *Ben* is meeting me at the party."

"What happened to Josh?"

"Nothing happened to him. We still go out occasionally, but we've never had an exclusive arrangement." She dangled a pink bag in front of her cousin's nose. "These go on before the dress."

She snatched the bag with a sigh. "I don't know why you and Ashley worried about finding the right bra for my dress. It's not like anyone would notice even if I wasn't wearing one."

"True. But it's not a bra, it's a bustier, and believe me, it will make everyone take notice," Paige promised.

Megan had never liked being the focus of attention and her cousin's response only made her more wary, but she shrugged out of her robe and, with Paige's assistance, into the black satin-and-lace undergarments her sister had carefully picked out for her.

"Now the dress," Paige said.

Megan wriggled into it.

"And the shoes."

She dutifully shoved her feet into the skyscraper-high heels—

"Jewelry."

—and added the chunky, silver earrings and necklace that Ann-Marie had picked out for her. The long chain meant that the teardrop-shaped pendant nestled in the hollow between her breasts, and when Megan glanced down at it, she was stunned.

"I have cleavage."

"Not much," Paige teased, "but some."

Megan turned to face the floor-length mirror that she rarely bothered to glance into and stared at her reflection. If not for the shell-shocked expression on the professionally made-up face that so perfectly depicted her feelings, she might have believed she was looking at a stranger.

The deep square neckline that had looked so simple and unassuming when she'd tried it on in the store now highlighted the swell of breasts she hadn't even realized she had. And the A-line, knee-length skirt showed off a lot of leg that, with the help of the three-inch heels, somehow looked more shapely than skinny.

Megan's hand went instinctively to the low neckline of the dress. "I can't go out in public looking like this."

Paige lifted a brow. "Like a beautiful, desirable woman?"

It wasn't such a stretch, Megan realized now, for someone to make that assumption. But she knew the truth, and the escalating panic inside of her confirmed it. "I can't," she said again. "It's not me."

"It is you," her cousin insisted. "Only dressed up a little on the outside."

Dressed up beyond recognition was more like it, but before she could say anything else, the doorbell chimed.

"That will be Gage," Paige guessed.

"Can you get it?" Megan pleaded with her. "I think I'm going to throw up."

Paige caught her arm as she turned toward the bathroom. "You're not going to throw up," she said firmly. "Now take a deep breath and go meet your date."

Megan went to the door, grumbling the whole way, and while her stomach was still in knots, the sound of the doorbell had caused them to loosen somewhat. No matter what other surprises or disasters the night might hold, at least he had shown up.

She took a deep breath and pulled open the door.

Gage was reaching forward to jab the button again when the door swung open. His lips started to curve in an automatic smile, then froze at the sight that greeted his eyes.

Megan?

The violet eyes confirmed her identity, even though they weren't hidden behind thick-framed glasses anymore. That was the most immediately obvious change, but not the only one. Her hair was different, too. Instead of being confined in the usual braid or ponytail, her long tresses had been fashioned into some kind of fancy twist, with a few strands left loose and curled to frame her face.

And how had he never noticed that she had such stunning features? Not just those fabulous eyes, but cheekbones that any cover model would die for and lips that made a man think of long, slow, deep kisses.

Then his gaze dipped lower, and his jaw nearly dropped when he realized that the dress she wore showcased curves that she'd kept well hidden beneath the boxy lab coats she wore at work. And the sexy heels made her mile-long legs look even longer.

When Gage had agreed to be Megan's date for tonight, he'd been prepared to go through the motions. He hadn't been prepared for the woman standing in front of him.

"Gage?" Her teeth sank into her bottom lip. A lip that was slicked with glossy color that brought to mind thoughts of a sun-ripened peach, making his mouth water. "Is something wrong?"

"No, um, nothing. It's just…I don't think I've ever seen you in a dress before." Against his will, his gaze drifted downward again.

"It's a push-up bra," she blurted out the explanation, then crossed her arms over her chest as her cheeks flooded with color.

But instead of hiding her newly revealed assets, the action only succeeded in pushing her breasts up farther, closer to the neckline, and enhancing his view. With great reluctance, he tore his gaze away.

"It, uh, they, I mean, *you* look great," he finally managed, and offered her the bouquet of purple tulips he'd kept concealed behind his back.

"You brought me flowers." He saw both surprise and pleasure in her eyes, heard them in her voice and wondered whether anyone had ever given her flowers before.

Gage shrugged. "I was walking by the florist and, when I saw them in the window, I thought of you."

"I love tulips, and these are beautiful." She uncrossed her arms and took the bouquet carefully, almost tentatively. "Thanks. I'll just go put them in some water."

He followed her inside, watched as she went through the routine of finding a vase, filling it with water, and arranging the flowers. It was a routine he'd watched dozens of women perform before, but he'd never seen anyone take such genuine pleasure in the task, find such joy in a simple gesture. Heck, a lot of the women he'd dated would have turned their noses up at the simple flowers because they weren't imported orchids or exotic calla lilies, and he was pleased that he'd gone with his instinct and bought the tulips.

Of course, his instincts now were pushing him in a whole different direction—toward the new and stunningly sexy Megan Roarke—but he managed to hold them in check. And if he couldn't help noticing how the skirt that hugged the sweet curve of her backside inched up a little as she leaned over to set the vase in the middle of the table, well, he was only human.

"I guess we should be going now," she said.

He yanked his mind back to the present. "Do you have a coat?"

She went to the closet, slid open the door.

Gage took the garment from her, holding it while she slipped the first arm in. As she turned to reach for the other sleeve, the side of her breast brushed his hand, and somehow that fleeting contact sent his blood humming.

He headed to the door, wondering and worrying about what other surprises the night might hold.

Chapter Five

Megan was feeling pretty good when Gage pulled into the long, winding driveway of the country club. The fact that the first awkward moments had passed allowed her to hope that the evening might not be a complete disaster. A feeling that dissipated with every step they took toward the doors.

Ashley had insisted that she wanted the engagement party to be an intimate gathering of family and close friends, but somehow the guest list had swelled so that nearly sixty people were expected to attend. And the number of cars in the parking lot suggested that most of them were already there.

The valet gave Gage a ticket, which he tucked into his pocket before reaching for Megan's hand, linking his warm fingers with her icy ones.

"Nervous?" he asked.

"It's silly, I know, but—" she halted at the bottom of

the steps "—this is probably a very bad idea. You've done nothing to deserve being subjected to my family."

"I've met your sister and your cousin," he reminded her. "They didn't seem so bad."

"They're mostly harmless," she agreed. "I can't say the same about everyone else."

"Every family tree has some baboons hanging from it."

She smiled at the analogy, but her smile faded when he tugged on her hand, leading her closer to the elaborately carved doors at the entrance.

"I've never brought a date to one of these events before," she felt compelled to confess.

"And you're worried that all your aunts, uncles and cousins will make a big deal out of the fact that you've brought one this time?"

She nodded.

"So why did you ask me to come?"

Because he sounded more curious than concerned, she answered honestly, "Because Paige dared me."

His smile was wry. "That hissing sound you hear is my ego deflating."

Her lips curved, just a little, as she shrugged. "I never expected that you would say yes."

"Are you sorry that I did?"

"No, but you might regret it."

He squared his shoulders. "You don't think I can handle your crazy uncle Wally?"

"As a matter of fact, I do have an uncle Wally," she told him. "But he lives in Canada. It's my great-aunt Vivian you need to watch out for."

"I appreciate the warning," Gage said, and squeezed her hand reassuringly. "Now let's join the party."

They were on their way to do just that after checking their coats when a cool voice said, "Excuse me, but the upstairs banquet room is closed for a private event."

Maybe she should have been flattered rather than annoyed that she hadn't been recognized, but annoyance won out, as it too often did when it came to dealing with members of Megan's family. "I know. It's my sister's engagement party."

The older woman's eyes popped wide-open and her mouth snapped shut. "Meg?"

"Yes, it's me, Aunt Viv." She dutifully kissed her aunt's dry, papery cheek.

"But where are your glasses?" Her gaze skimmed over her niece with obvious disapproval. "And your clothes?" Then shifted to Gage. "And who is this?"

And so it begins, Megan thought, but managed to hold back her sigh.

"This is Gage Richmond," she said. Then, to Gage, "My great-aunt, Vivian Roarke."

"Richmond," she said, and narrowed her gaze. "As in Pharmaceuticals?"

Before Gage could respond, Lillian glided down the stairs in a cloud of flowing silk and sweet perfume.

"There you are, Megan." Lillian smiled at her daughter. "Your sister was just wondering what was keeping you."

Megan couldn't remember ever having been so grateful for her mother's interruption, despite the subtle censure in her statement.

Then her mother looked at Gage and smiled. "Although I think I've found the answer to that question."

It wasn't quite so easy to hold back her sigh this time. "Mom, this is Gage Richmond. Gage, my mother, Lillian."

"A pleasure to meet you," Gage said.

"The pleasure is mine," Lillian said. "And I'm so grateful you're here with Megan this evening."

It was an effort to keep the smile on her face, to pretend her mother's comment hadn't been a slap in the face.

Of course Lillian was *grateful* for Gage's presence— it allowed her to pretend, at least for one night, that her daughter wasn't a complete social misfit, who never had a date for family events.

"If you'll excuse me," Megan said, to no one in particular, "I'm going to find Ashley."

Gage caught up with her at the top of the stairs. "You weren't trying to abandon me down there, were you?"

"Haven't you ever heard the expression 'every man for himself'?" she asked.

"Sure," he agreed, reaching for her hand. "Except that tonight I'm here for *you*. Whatever you need."

He stroked his thumb across her knuckles. Megan's eyes widened and the pulse at the base of her throat jumped.

He hadn't really thought about what he was doing, hadn't intended to change the rules of their game, but suddenly, there was an awareness simmering between them that hadn't been there before. Or maybe it just hadn't been acknowledged.

She swallowed. "All I need is a couple hours of your time." Her gaze darted away from his, but not before he saw the nerves lurking beneath the surface. "And maybe a glass of wine."

He could use a drink himself, and was grateful to see that there wasn't much of a line at the bar. "Red or white?" he asked her.

"Oh. I didn't mean—you don't have to—"

"Red or white?" he asked again.

Her cheeks flushed. "Red."

He gave her hand a friendly squeeze before releasing it. "I'll be right back."

She watched him make his way toward the bar, and wondered if she'd imagined the zing she'd felt when he held her hand, and the heat she'd seen in his eyes when they'd locked on hers.

She saw her cousin Camilla in line in front of Gage, and she turned slightly to speak to him, smiling flirtatiously and laughing at whatever he'd said in response.

Yes, she'd definitely imagined it, because Gage Richmond couldn't possibly be attracted to her—not when a woman like Camilla was around.

When the bartender gave Camilla her drink, she fluttered her fingertips at Gage before moving away.

"You can thank me later."

Megan turned to Paige. "For what?"

"The fact that you got a pedicure *and* a gorgeous date for the evening."

"You made sure the former was contingent on the latter," Megan reminded her. "But speaking of dates…?"

"Ben's on his way," Paige said. "He got caught up at the office."

"On a Saturday?"

"He's got an important deposition on Monday."

"You've got to start dating men in another profession."

"Where would I ever meet any?"

"You're asking me?"

Paige glanced toward the bar again. "Hey, does Gage have a brother?"

"He does. Married."

"Damn."

Megan chuckled.

"Oh, double damn," Paige muttered, and grabbed Megan's arm. "Gage is in trouble."

She turned and winced. Gage might have survived his encounter with cousin Camilla, but now Aunt Vivian had moved in. "If he comes back after a one-on-one with Aunt Viv instead of bolting for the door, I'll be surprised."

"Forget surprised," Paige said. "I'd snap him up and never let him go."

Megan shook her head regretfully, because she knew that wasn't an option.

While he was waiting at the bar, Gage noticed that Megan's cousin, Paige, had joined her, so he ordered a drink for her, too. And when he turned away with his hands full, he found himself confronted by Megan's elderly aunt.

The older woman's brightly painted lips curved. "Gage, wasn't it? I was hoping we'd have a chance to chat."

"Really?" he said. "About what?"

"Oh, I just wanted to make sure that Megan was taking good care of you."

"I have no complaints," he assured her.

"Has she introduced you to my granddaughter, Camilla?" Vivian nodded in the direction of the attractive blonde who'd chatted him up while he was waiting in line, and whom he'd noticed had guzzled down her gin and tonic like it was water.

"No, but we met," he told her.

"I was so pleased to see her here tonight," she confided. "I was so worried that she wouldn't want to come, since she just broke up with her boyfriend."

She paused, as if to give him a chance to respond. Since he had no idea what kind of response was appropriate, he remained silent.

"He was a college professor," the elderly woman

continued. "It was a messy split, very unfortunate. But I'm sure she'll find someone else.

"She's a lovely girl—and smart. Graduated cum laude with a degree in art history from the Weinberg College of Arts & Sciences at Northwestern."

He nodded politely. "Megan went to Northwestern, too, didn't she?"

Vivian nodded, though her scowl warned that she didn't appreciate the reminder.

Of course, she wouldn't, because Gage knew that Megan had graduated *summa* cum laude with a master's in science, which more than trumped Camilla's accomplishment.

"Megan always had brains," Vivian acknowledged, with more than a hint of reluctance. "That was apparent at an early age. And a good thing, too, because she was a homely child, and had no idea how to relate to other children her own age."

Gage stared at her. "You do know that you're talking about my date?"

She waved a hand. "As if anyone would believe a man like you could be seriously interested in Megan."

"A man like me?"

"Handsome. Successful. Sophisticated."

Rich.

Of course, she wasn't crass enough to mention his financial status, but he'd seen the gleam in her eye when she'd caught his last name. A gleam that he'd seen in far too many eyes in his thirty-two years, but never in Megan's. Whatever reasons she had for inviting him to be here tonight, it wasn't because she had visions of landing a wealthy husband.

And as uncertain as he'd been about his reasons for agreeing to this "date" in the first place, he was enjoying being with Megan. Sure, she was more introverted than the women he usually dated, but once she'd started to open up, he found himself really enjoying her company.

She was kind and generous and insightful—and smart. He'd never concerned himself with a woman's mind before. So long as his date was attractive and fun and knew that he wasn't looking for anything long-term, she was his kind of woman.

Megan was different. She was attractive—a lot more so than he'd suspected. And it wasn't just the mile-long legs or the unexpected curves put on display by the dress she was wearing. It was the capability of those slender shoulders, the strength in her delicate hands and the mystery of those stunning eyes.

"And Megan is beautiful, smart and talented," he said, searching for—and finding her—across the room. "So why is it you think a man like me wouldn't be interested in a woman like her?"

As if sensing his stare, Megan turned and caught his eye. Her lips curved, just a little, and something inside of him stirred, responded.

There was no longer any doubt in his mind that—if circumstances were different—she was a woman he could be interested in. But he had his eyes on a bigger prize and so he reminded himself that all he wanted from Megan was her cooperation with respect to his plan.

Okay, maybe that wasn't all he *wanted,* but it was all he needed. And he wouldn't let himself forget that.

"Now if you'll excuse me," Gage said, not caring whether she did or not, "I'd like to get back to my date."

Megan and Gage found an empty table on the edge of the dance floor and settled in with their drinks. Paige came by to introduce her date when Ben finally arrived, and the four of them chatted for a while, but their conversation was continuously interrupted by friends and family who stopped by the table on the pretense of wanting to say hello to Megan.

But she knew the truth—they all wanted the scoop on Gage. And while she knew she'd brought this on herself by inviting him, she decided she'd rather be thought of as "poor lonely Megan" than attract this kind of unwanted attention.

But Gage was a good sport about it. And he had the grace to pretend he was oblivious when other women tried to flirt with him—while Megan was sitting right beside him. Of course, that only proved what she already knew, that no one believed he could be seriously interested in her.

So lost was she in these thoughts that she jolted when he put a hand on her arm.

"Do you want to dance?"

She hadn't realized the band had begun to play until he asked, and as tempted as she was by the desire to be held in his arms, her desire to fade in the background was still stronger. "I'd rather not."

"Why not?"

"I'm not a very good dancer."

"Then think of it as practice." He pushed back his chair. "Because you'll have to dance at the wedding."

"I really don't—" From the corner of her eye, she saw her mother moving in their direction. With a resigned sigh, Megan took his proffered hand and rose to her feet.

He smiled. "You were saying?"

"I don't think I've ever had a better offer," she ad-libbed.

The sparkle in his eye told her that he knew exactly why she'd changed her mind, but he made no further comment.

Gage was a great dancer, which didn't surprise Megan in the least. She imagined that anything Gage Richmond chose to do, he did well.

It made her wonder—if only for a moment—what it would be like to make love with him. No doubt he would be very, very good at that, but she quickly shoved that fantasy aside before it had a chance to go any further.

"Relax." Gage murmured the word close to her ear. "Block out everything else but the sound of the music."

His breath was warm on her cheek, his tone soothing. But Megan could barely hear the music over the pounding of her heart, the rush of the blood in her veins.

"I'm not very comfortable in crowds," she said, because it was true and because it was easier to admit that than to reveal that every nerve ending in her body was on high alert because of *him*.

"Forget the crowd," he told her. "There's just you and me."

If he was trying to get her to relax, that certainly wasn't going to do it.

Conversation, she decided, would be safer than letting her imagination run wild.

"I got the memo about the staff meeting on Monday," she said.

"No shoptalk on a date," Gage chided gently.

She frowned. "Then what are we supposed to talk about?"

"Anything but work."

Which was easy to say, but Megan didn't really know how to talk about anything else. "So, how about those Yankees?"

Gage chuckled.

"What?"

"It's the beginning of March."

"So?"

"They're still in spring training in Florida."

"Oh."

"And anyway, I'm a BoSox fan."

"Really?"

"Five years at Harvard made an impression," he told her. "Which makes baseball a taboo subject at family dinners."

"Your dad and your brother are both Yankees fans?" she guessed.

"They are," he agreed. "But neither of them are as devoted as my sister-in-law."

"So what do you talk about at family dinners?" she wondered.

"Anything else. Although with four kids around the table, any kind of conversation can be difficult."

"It sounds like you're close to your family."

"Aren't you?"

She considered the question for a moment before responding. "To my sister, yes. And Paige is like a second sister. But my mom?" She shook her head. "We just seem to have different ideas about everything. In particular, she's never understood why I believe my work is more important than finding a husband."

"I get the same thing from my family. Not that they want me to find a husband—" he grinned "—but they do think I would benefit from settling down."

She was surprised that he was telling her this. Then she realized that he was telling her because she was safe, because she didn't have any illusions that he was talking about settling down with her.

"What do you think?" she asked him.

"I don't think I'm the settling type," he told her. "Although my father insists that I just haven't been dating the right kind of woman."

"I wouldn't have guessed there was a kind you'd missed."

She dropped her head, mortified by what she'd just said.

But Gage only chuckled as he led her off of the dance floor when the song finished. "You don't pull any punches, do you?"

"I didn't mean—"

"Yes, you did," he refuted, clearly unoffended. "And it's okay. I *have* dated a lot of women."

"I was surprised you didn't already have plans when I asked you to come here tonight," she admitted.

He shrugged as he drew her out onto the balcony. "I've taken a break from the social scene the last couple of months."

"I guess the rumor mill has been kept busy recycling old news, then."

"Of course, there will be all kinds of new gossip now that we're an item."

"We're not…" she began, then realized he was teasing.

"Maybe we're not," he agreed. "But you don't have to sound appalled at the prospect of having your name linked with mine."

"I didn't mean it like that."

"What did you mean?"

"Just that no one would ever believe we were a couple."

He thought about what her aunt had said to him earlier, and her misguided matchmaking attempts. "You're right. We definitely need to work on that."

"How?"

"For starters, it would help if you didn't freeze up every time I touched you," Gage told her. "Just relax."

"Relax? Around those people?"

He smiled. "I don't think your family is the biggest problem."

"That's because they're not *your* family," she muttered.

He settled his hands on her shoulders.

She stilled, every muscle in her body going rigid.

"That's what I'm talking about," he said.

"What?" she asked, feigning ignorance.

He tugged her closer.

Her heart pounded harder.

He dipped his head and whispered close to her ear.

"You could at least pretend you're happy to be alone with me."

Happy was hardly the word she would use to describe how she was feeling. Surprised. Confused. Aroused. Oh, yeah, *definitely* aroused.

What was it about this man that sent her hormones rocketing like Fourth of July firecrackers? And all he'd done was put his hands on her shoulders. Okay, his hands were moving now, stroking down her arms, and slowly upward again, sending tingles through her whole body.

"Except that we're not entirely alone," he admitted softly.

"What?" She knew it was his proximity that was wreaking havoc with her ability to concentrate on his words, the tantalizing scent of him teasing her nostrils, taunting her hormones.

"Your cousin Camilla. She's standing next to that potted palm beside the door, pretending not to watch us."

"That sounds like something she would do," Megan admitted, more than a little irritated that her cousin was lurking in the shadows, probably waiting to catch Gage alone so she could hit on him.

"Maybe we should give her something to talk about." He lowered his head toward her.

"I appreciate what you're doing," she said. "But I think—"

"Stop thinking," he said, and brushed his lips gently against hers.

So gently, and so briefly, that Megan wasn't sure the contact had even happened.

"Just for two minutes," he said, "stop thinking, stop worrying about your family and concentrate on this."

Then he kissed her again—and she melted like the chocolate fondue on the dessert table.

She'd been kissed before. She'd been touched and groped and she'd had sex. She might not be a woman of vast experience, but she wasn't innocent. At least, she hadn't thought so.

But she'd never been kissed like Gage was kissing her.

She could taste the beer he'd drank, and something else—an elemental male flavor that went straight to her bloodstream and made her head spin and her knees tremble.

Then his hands slipped around her waist, drew her nearer. She could feel the heat and strength of his palms even through the fabric of her dress, and she found herself wondering how they would feel on her bare skin. Even knowing it was a fantasy that could never come true didn't stop her from thinking about it, wanting it, wanting *him*.

Her lips parted on a sigh, and his tongue dipped inside. A lazy stroke, gently teasing, hotly tempting.

This was wrong. She shouldn't be doing this. She certainly shouldn't be pouring her heart and her soul into a kiss that wasn't intended to mean anything. Or maybe it was just long-dormant hormones reawakened. Whatever the reason, Megan was helpless to resist the seduction of his kiss.

She felt as if she was drunk on champagne, though she'd only had a single glass of wine. Her heart was pounding, her blood was pulsing and her body was filled with a yearning she didn't think she'd ever experienced before.

His hands slid slowly up her back, then down again.

It had been so long since she'd had a man's hands on her, and Gage's felt good, so good.

And then his hands stopped moving and his lips eased away from her.

"Well, that should give your cousin something to think about."

Cousin?

Megan blinked the clouds from her eyes.

Right. He'd kissed her because he knew Camilla was watching them, because he was helping her fool her family into believing they were really a couple. But for a minute there, it had seemed so real, so perfect. And she should have known it was too perfect to be real.

She took a step back, giving herself some physical space while she drew in a deep breath and reined in her rampant hormones.

Thank goodness it was only an act—she wouldn't stand a hope of resisting him if he ever truly turned his attentions in her direction.

"Meg?"

She pushed those thoughts aside and turned her attention back to her date.

"Are you ready to go back inside?" he asked.

She managed a smile. "Sure."

* * *

Gage was careful not to touch Megan as he followed her back into the dining room, careful to remind himself that the kiss was just for show. A calculated move to convince Megan's nosy cousin to mind her own business. It wasn't supposed to mean anything. And it sure as hell wasn't supposed to leave him wanting a lot more.

But looking at her now, at her flushed cheeks and swollen lips, he couldn't deny the want and hunger that stirred inside of him. Completely unexpected—and undeniably real.

"I seem to recall something being said about food," he commented, as if the ache in his belly could be assuaged by some crackers and brie.

"Hot and cold hors d'oeuvres," Megan said, glancing over at the crowd around the buffet table. "Or we could skip out and go somewhere else to grab a burger and fries."

He smiled at the hopeful tone in her voice. "What would your sister say about you skipping out?"

"It's not like I would tell her."

"Don't you think she'd notice?"

She sighed. "Yeah, Ashley probably would."

He heard what she didn't say—Ashley would notice but no one else would.

She was obviously used to being overlooked, ignored. And he suspected that she might even prefer it that way. Still, it had to rankle a little that most of her family seemed to think she was below their notice. It certainly rankled him on her behalf.

He frowned at that, recognizing that he was venturing into dangerous territory with Megan. Or maybe it wasn't dangerous territory at all. Maybe the urge to protect her from the criticisms and insensitivity of her family was similar to what a brother would feel for his sister.

Not having a sister, he couldn't say for sure. But he did know that he would never have kissed a sister the way he'd kissed Megan. And he wouldn't be thinking about kissing her again, wanting to devour the softest, sweetest mouth he'd ever tasted. No, it definitely wasn't a brotherly thing, and he had no idea how to handle this new and unexpected complication.

He took a plate and began piling it with fancy little appetizers that were more likely to whet than satisfy his appetite. But it was safer to stay here, surrounded by Megan's family and friends, than to be alone with her right now. "I'll take a rain check on the burger, if that's okay."

Megan was silent as she studied the display of coconut shrimp. Or maybe she was silent because Vivian had joined the line at the buffet table and she didn't want her elderly aunt overhearing their conversation—a suspicion that proved true when they were seated and she finally responded to his question.

"I appreciate that you're here with me," she said. "But we both know that you only agreed to come because you felt as if you owed me a favor. Now you don't."

"And your point?" he prompted, popping a stuffed mushroom in his mouth.

"My point—" she swirled a carrot stick in the dip she'd spooned onto the edge of her plate "—is that there's no reason to talk about rain checks because there's no reason for us to ever see one another outside of the lab again."

"What if I want to see you again?"

She bit off the end of the carrot, then stared at him, clearly baffled by the possibility. And he found himself again mesmerized by those wide, violet eyes.

She chewed, swallowed, then finally asked, "Why would you?"

He fought against a smile. "Forgetting the *why* for a moment, it seems that I do."

She considered that while she nibbled on the rest of her carrot stick.

"I'm not easy," she told him. "Despite the way I wrapped myself around you on the terrace, I'm not going to sleep with you."

He'd never known a woman who just blurted out what she was thinking the way that Megan did. After dating so many women who played mind games or worked personal agendas, her forthrightness was refreshing—and only one of the things he was beginning to like about her.

"I'd say the wrapping was mutual, and while I certainly wouldn't object to more of the same, it wasn't my plan to take you to bed."

Of course, that hadn't stopped him from thinking along those lines when her body was pressed against his, but the fact that they worked together complicated the situation immeasurably. Not to mention that she could be exactly what he needed to secure the promotion that his father had dangled in front of him like a proverbial carrot.

But as he watched the little furrow between her brows deepen, he couldn't resist saying, "Not yet, anyway."

Chapter Six

Megan was enjoying her first cup of coffee and the quiet solitude of the morning when she heard a key in the lock. A glance at the clock revealed that it wasn't quite ten—earlier than her sister usually came home after spending the night with her fiancé, and a lot earlier than she would have expected the morning after their engagement celebration.

And when Ashley came into the kitchen, Megan noticed that Paige was right behind her.

"Why are you home so early? And what are you doing here?" The first question being directed to her sister and the second to her cousin.

"Are you kidding me?" Paige responded first. "I saw the lip-lock on the terrace."

"And I want to hear all the details," Ashley demanded.

Megan took a long sip of her coffee, hoping the oversize mug hid the flush in her cheeks. "It was an Academy-worthy performance, wasn't it?"

Her sister scowled as she put on the kettle for the tea she favored. "What do you mean 'performance'?"

"Gage was there, *pretending* to be my boyfriend," she reminded her sister and cousin. "He thought a kiss might further the illusion."

"A kiss is a way of testing the waters," Paige said. "Like dipping a toe in the ocean. You and Gage—that was a tsunami."

"It really wasn't that big of a deal," she denied, while secretly agreeing that in Gage's arms, she'd felt as if she'd been swamped by an enormous wave. The heat and hunger had crashed over her, dragging her into depths that were so far over her head she wasn't sure she would ever find solid ground again.

But it had only been one kiss.

Despite having alluded to wanting to do that and a whole lot more, when he took her home, he simply walked her to her door, took the keys from her hand to unlock it for her, then stepped back and said "Good night, Megan."

And she'd gone inside alone, uncertain whether she should be relieved or disappointed.

"Then you've been getting a lot more action than I have." Paige's complaint drew her attention back to the present. "Because I got seared from the heat standing on the edge of the terrace."

"And I missed it," Ashley grumbled.

"You've got your own hot-and-heavy romance," Paige reminded her. "I'm the one who needs to live vicariously."

"Things didn't go well with Ben last night?" Megan asked, anxious to change the topic of conversation.

Her cousin shrugged. "He's sexy and sweet, but there just isn't any zing."

Before last night, Megan wouldn't have had a clue what she meant. She'd been attracted to other men, had experienced the stirring of desire, but nothing in the category of zing. But after last night, after being held in Gage's arms, she definitely knew about zing.

When Megan came into the lab Monday morning, Gage noted that she'd gone back to wearing her glasses.

And the ponytail and baggy clothes.

He was a little disappointed, but not really surprised. He wasn't sure if she felt more comfortable dressed that way, or if she deliberately downplayed her natural attractiveness so that she didn't draw attention to herself.

If he had to guess, he would say it was the latter, and he couldn't deny that her efforts were mostly successful. He certainly hadn't taken much notice of her prior to their chance encounter at the shopping mall.

But now that he knew her a little better, was aware of the subtle curves hiding beneath her clothes and the unexpected passion simmering beneath her cool demeanor, he knew he would never be able to look at her the same way again.

He would never be able to look into her eyes and not remember how they'd gone all misty and soft—like lavender fog—when he'd held her in his arms. And he'd never be able to look at her mouth and not remember how soft and sweet it tasted, and how avidly it had responded to his kiss.

But if memories of their kiss had tormented him throughout the rest of the weekend, Megan gave no indication that it had even happened. As always, she was the consummate professional at work. She performed the tasks that were assigned to her, answered questions when they were asked and generally continued with her duties as usual. She never sought him out, never initiated conversation, and not once did he catch her looking in his direction—as he found himself looking in hers, a lot.

He let her continue to ignore him—as it was obvious to him that's what she was doing—for three whole weeks. On Friday at the end of the third week, as they were clearing up in preparation of leaving for the weekend, he finally approached her.

Megan looked up from the stack of files she was sorting. "I can finish up here if you have to go."

"Go where?"

She shrugged. "It's a Friday night. I thought you might have plans."

He shook his head. "The only women I've seen since we've started prepping for this trial are the clinical subjects. And you."

"Did you lose your little black book?" she teased.

A few weeks earlier, he couldn't have imagined that she would have teased him about anything, and he wouldn't have guessed that she had a sense of humor. But he knew her better now—and still not nearly as well as he wanted to know her.

"It's a BlackBerry," he teased back, and earned one of those rare, shy smiles. "But the only reason I'm anxious to get out of here tonight is that I'm hungry."

"Me, too," she admitted.

"Got any plans for dinner?" he asked, deliberately casual.

"Oh, um, no," she said. "Nothing specific. But I wasn't fishing for an invitation or anything like that."

"I know," he said. "But I'm in the mood for a burger and I have a rain check to cash in."

Megan finished unbuttoning her lab coat, hung it on the hook by the door. "Actually, I'm—"

"You're not going to renege on your promise, are you?"

"I don't recall making a promise."

"Then it's a good thing I do."

And that's how they ended up at The Ranch with plates overloaded with quarter-pound burgers and spicy spiral fries. They didn't talk much while they ate, or not about anything of significance, and when Gage finally pushed his empty plate aside, he noticed that Megan had nearly cleaned hers, too.

"You have an impressive appetite for a skinny little thing," he noted.

"I like food," she admitted. "It just never seems to stick."

"What else do you like?"

She nibbled on a fry. "What do you mean—like books, music, movies?"

"Sure, we can start there."

She sipped at her cola—the regular kind, not diet. "I'll read almost anything, though I lean toward nonfiction."

"Music?" he prompted.

"Blues-rock."

"Movies?"

"Anything that I don't have to think too much about. If I'm going to spend twenty bucks, which is what it costs by the time you add a bag of popcorn and a soda to the price of the ticket, I want to enjoy it. No dark war settings or depressing social issues or complicated psychological thrillers."

"If it was my twenty bucks, could I pick the show?"

She frowned over his question as she sipped her cola again. "Are you inviting me to a movie?"

"Well, you did spring for dinner," he said. "And there's a new Vin Diesel movie playing. You know the kind, with lots of car chases and big explosions and very little plot."

"Sounds like my kind of entertainment," she said.

"Then it's a date."

* * *

She was okay until he called it a date.

Grabbing a bite to eat with a coworker—even if that coworker was Gage Richmond—wasn't a big deal. Deciding to catch a movie together because they both had nothing else to do shouldn't have been, either. But as soon as Gage put that label on it, all of her perceptions changed, and the easy camaraderie they'd been sharing suddenly wasn't so easy anymore.

Unfortunately, she'd already agreed, and as the movie theater was within the same shopping complex as the restaurant, she had neither the time nor the opportunity to come up with a reason to bow out. He took her hand as they walked across the parking lot and Megan tried to be as nonchalant as he was about it, as if she held hands with guys all the time, as if the casual contact didn't make her pulse race.

Gage was standing in line at one of the automated kiosks to buy their tickets when Megan felt vibrations in her chest. At first she thought it was her heart knocking erratically against her ribs, then she remembered that her cell phone was tucked in the inside pocket of her jacket and set to vibrate.

"Excuse me," she said to Gage, and stepped away to answer the call.

"I know you had to work late tonight," Ashley said without preamble. "I just wondered if you could pick up some Motrin on your way home."

"What's wrong?" Megan asked, alerted not just by the request for the medication but the obvious strain in her sister's voice.

"The usual," Ashley said, then sucked in a breath, and blew it out again. "Okay, it's hit a little bit harder than usual."

She moved back to Gage, who had just started scrolling through the movie options on the screen. "I'll be home in fifteen minutes," she promised.

Gage looked up and, without any question, stepped away from the machine so the next person in line could proceed.

"Problem?" he asked.

"My sister's not feeling well."

"Anything I can do to help?"

She shook her head. "Thanks, but no. You can stay and watch car chases, but I have to get home."

"Rain check?"

"That's really not—"

He touched his finger to her lips, halting her protest.

"Rain check," he said again, and it wasn't a question this time.

"Okay."

He insisted on walking her to her car, told her to take care of her sister and watched her pull out of the parking lot.

And though she was anxious to get home to Ashley, she didn't quite manage to banish all thoughts of Gage from her mind as she drove away. And she couldn't completely extinguish the little flicker of hope that the interest she'd seen in his eyes could be real.

At home, Megan found her sister on the sofa in the living room, curled up under a blanket and obviously in pain.

When Ashley had first been diagnosed with endometriosis, she'd been willing to try anything that might relieve the pain. It turned out that her symptoms could be treated quite successfully through the use of oral contraceptives. The problem with that, of course, was that she wouldn't get pregnant so long as she was taking them.

Megan suspected that was why Ashley was suffering now, that she'd stopped taking her pills. It was no secret that her sister wanted a baby and while pregnancy happened easily for many women, it wouldn't be easy for Ashley. In fact, her doctors had warned that it might not happen for her at all, but she refused to give up on the dream of someday holding a child of her own in her arms.

"Hey," Megan said, coming into the room.

Ashley managed a weak smile as she accepted the medication and the glass of water her sister held out to her. "Thanks."

Megan lowered herself onto the coffee table. "What's going on, Ash? You haven't had pain like this in years."

Her sister dropped her gaze. "I stopped taking the Pill."

Though it was just what she'd expected, Megan couldn't hold back her sigh. "When? Why?"

"Just a few weeks ago. Because Trevor and I are getting married in the fall anyway and because I really want a baby." Tears spilled onto her cheeks and she swiped at them impatiently. "And maybe because I feel him slipping away and I don't know why, but I know if I get pregnant it will make things better."

Megan wasn't so sure that was the answer, but she was hardly in a position to offer relationship counseling to anyone. "Why didn't you talk to me about this?" she asked instead.

"Because I didn't think it was fair to always run to my little sister with my problems."

"Forget the big and little part. You're my sister."

"I'm sorry I pulled you away from the lab."

This time it was Megan who looked away. "I wasn't actually at the lab."

"Where were you?"

"I just went to grab a bite to eat."

"Based on the deliberate vagueness of that response, I'm guessing you didn't go alone," Ashley said. "In fact, I'm guessing that you were with Gage."

"So?"

"So…good for you."

Megan frowned. "You're making a big deal out of something that isn't."

"Maybe. Maybe not." Her sister managed a smile. "I'm sorry I ruined your dinner."

"You didn't." Megan jumped up when the microwave dinged, grateful for the reprieve from her sister's questioning. She came back with a warm bean bag, which she laid gently across Ashley's abdomen.

"Thanks."

"Can I get you anything else?" Megan asked. "Do you want me to call Trevor?"

Ashley shook her head. "I tried calling him before I called you. I tried his office and his cell and got his voice mail both times."

"You knew he was working late tonight," Megan pointed out reasonably. "It makes sense that he would turn his phone off if he was with a client."

Her sister nodded, though she didn't look convinced. "You're right. It's just that he's seemed so distracted and inaccessible over the last few weeks."

"It's tax season," Megan reminded her.

"You're right," she said again.

"Do you want a cup of tea?" Megan asked, hoping a mug of chai and a change of subject would smooth the furrow in her sister's brow.

Ashley shook her head. "I want to hear more about your date with Gage."

It was a change of subject but not quite the one Megan was hoping for.

"It wasn't a date."

Her sister's brows lifted. "You were having dinner with a man yummier than anything on the menu—what would you call it?"

"A burger and fries."

Ashley shook her head. "You wouldn't have had the nerve to ask him out again—not without some serious bribery or blackmail being involved—so he must have invited you. Which means, obviously, that he's interested."

"Or maybe he just didn't want to eat alone. You said it yourself," Megan reminded her. "Gage is like the yummiest thing on the menu—the juiciest sirloin burger with all of the fixings. I'm the pickle spear they throw on the side of the plate. No one really wants it and it's not particularly appealing, but it takes up space."

"That's so not true," Ashley objected, then sucked in her breath and gritted her teeth.

Megan, understanding that another wave of pain had hit, turned the bean bag over. "Okay?"

Ashley nodded, exhaled slowly. "How are preparations for the trial going?"

"They're under way," Megan said, relieved to abandon the topic of Gage Richmond for now. "We're scheduled to begin administration of the drug to the first group next weekend."

She didn't often talk to her sister about her work, partly because Ashley had no interest in what she was talking about. But a couple years earlier, she'd started doing some independent research in the hope of finding a drug that would not just help alleviate the symptoms of endometriosis for women who were trying to have children but improve their chances of conception.

About a year earlier, when she'd finally made some progress, she'd taken it to her boss at Richmond Pharmaceuticals and received official approval—and a budget—to continue her research. And now the drug whose development she had spearheaded was going into the clinical-trial phase.

"When will you know if it works?" Ashley asked, obviously anxious for some good news.

"It's hard to say," Megan told her. "The subjects will undergo testing at prescribed intervals throughout the next twelve months."

"A whole year?"

Megan knew her sister felt as if she'd been waiting for forever already, and to wait another twelve months seemed interminable.

"Well," Ashley said philosophically. "At least you have a reason to look forward to going into work every day."

"I've always enjoyed my job," Megan reminded her. "But, yes, I am anxious to see the results of this trial."

Her sister smiled. "I wasn't referring to the trial. I was referring to you spending a lot more time with Gage Richmond."

Megan refused to admit how much she was looking forward to that. Because she would never hear the end of it if her sister had the slightest clue about how hard and how fast her heart beat whenever Gage was near, how her knees got weak if he stood close, and how everything inside of her felt all hot and quivery if he so much as smiled at her.

No way would Megan admit any of that to her sister. She wasn't sure she was ready to admit it even to herself.

Chapter Seven

It had been years since Gage had worried about asking a woman out on a date. Maybe he'd been spoiled in that it was rare for an invitation he'd issued—be it for dinner or dancing or a more private evening—to be refused. Or maybe he hadn't really cared one way or the other. When he thought about calling Megan Saturday afternoon, though, he was unexpectedly apprehensive.

But he'd promised her a rain check, and he intended to deliver. Of course, she might already have plans, and he could accept that. Or she might simply not want to go out with him, but he didn't want to acknowledge that was a possibility.

When the phone rang, he was both annoyed and relieved by the interruption. He snatched up the receiver. "Hello?"

"Gage Richmond, it must be my lucky day that I managed to catch you at home."

The sultry feminine voice was vaguely familiar, but Gage was having trouble filling in the details. "Who is this?"

The laugh was rich and warm. "I should be offended that you have to ask, but it has been a while. It's Norah Hennesy."

Norah Hennesy.

Tall…dark hair…luscious curves…and very, very flexible.

They'd dated for a few months more than two years earlier, and had gone their separate ways when she grew frustrated by Gage's refusal to commit.

"It has been a while," he agreed.

"Much too long."

Gage didn't need to be hit over the head to figure out why she was calling. And while he'd occasionally rekindled affairs with ex-lovers in the past, he wasn't in the mood to go another round in the mating game with a partner who was looking toward a radically different finish line.

"So I was thinking," Norah continued, "that we could maybe get some dinner at Chez Henri and get reacquainted."

Chez Henri was an exclusive and expensive French restaurant where they'd frequently dined in the past. Gage had never quite figured out if Norah liked the food as much as she liked being seen there, but he'd never objected because the restaurant was close to Norah's apartment and dinner had inevitably led to drinks back at her place and, if he felt like staying, breakfast in the morning.

It had been a long time since he'd had…breakfast with a woman, but her offer did little to pique his interest. Or maybe it was the fact that when he tried to picture the slumberous and satisfied morning-after look in her eyes—he simply couldn't. Because he couldn't remember the color of her eyes. He only knew that they weren't violet.

Whoa—where had that thought come from?

"Gage?"

He forced his attention back to the woman on the other end of the phone. "That's a tempting offer," he lied, "but I already have plans for tonight."

"Oh." He could hear the disappointment in her voice. "Maybe another time?"

"Actually, I don't think so, Norah."

"You're seeing someone," she guessed.

He started to deny it, but then he thought of Megan again. "Yeah, I am."

"Well, then, maybe I'll try again in a few weeks," she said.

He frowned at her response, at this confirmation that everyone knew his reputation, and that no one ever expected his relationships to last—least of all Gage himself.

Even after he ended the call, he wondered how to define his relationship with Megan, or even if it could be called a relationship. She was a coworker, and maybe she was becoming a friend, but beneath everything else was an underlying physical attraction that was as baffling as it was intriguing.

He'd never known anyone like her—sweet and sexy and blissfully oblivious to her own appeal. And maybe it was this uniqueness that fascinated him.

Not that he had any intention of getting himself all tied up in knots over a woman just because she had eyes that haunted him in his sleep and lips that were so soft and sweet and so incredibly and passionately responsive.

No way. Especially not with the vice-presidency on the line.

He picked up the phone again and dialed her number, anyway.

Megan was caught off guard by Gage's phone call. It was the only excuse she had for saying yes when he asked if she wanted to catch the movie they'd missed a couple of weeks earlier.

Still, she hated that she was a nervous wreck waiting for him to show up. In the lab, she wasn't quite so intimidated by him because they were on a more equal footing. Over the past few weeks, she'd gradually become accustomed to working closely with him. But outside of the lab, she was all too aware of how completely out of her league she was with him.

"You're not wearing your glasses," he commented when she answered the door.

"My sister stepped on them, snapped the arm off."

And Megan wasn't convinced it had been an accident. Of course, Ashley denied that she'd broken them on purpose, but in the next breath she'd accused her sister of hiding behind the thick lenses and claimed she'd done her a favor by breaking them. Whether Ashley's actions had been intentional or not, the end result was that Megan had to put her contacts in if she was going to see anything.

"How is your sister?" he asked now.

"She's feeling much better."

"Was it that nasty cold that's going around?"

She shook her head. "No, it was just, uh, a female thing."

"Oh," Gage replied and, thankfully, left it at that.

Uncomfortable with the direction of the conversation, Megan ducked her head and lifted a hand to push her glasses up. Then she remembered they weren't there and rubbed a finger over the bridge of her nose, as if to assuage an itch. But the corners of Gage's mouth lifted, and she knew she hadn't fooled him.

"I don't wear contacts very often," she admitted. "So I keep trying to push up glasses that aren't even there."

"I like when you wear your contacts," Gage said. "It's easier to see your eyes."

She dropped her gaze again.

"You have beautiful eyes, Megan."

She felt her cheeks flame. "Thank you," she managed to respond.

"And lips so soft a man can sink right into them."

She absolutely would not get all weak and flustered just because that smooth, sexy voice tempted a woman to forget all reason. "How many lines like that have you memorized for the sole purpose of making a woman go all warm and quivery inside?"

He only smiled. "Are you all warm and quivery inside?"

She was hot and trembling and very close to melting into a puddle at his feet. Recognizing that fact, she drew in a deep, calming breath and moved away to pick up her purse. "Yes, but Vin Diesel always has that effect on me."

Gage chuckled. "I guess that put me in my place."

But the real problem for Megan was that his place was right beside her through the movie.

He did his best to make her comfortable, keeping the conversation light and easy while they waited for the feature to begin. It wasn't his fault that her heart sped up when the lights dimmed, or that her pulse raced when his fingers brushed against hers inside the tub of popcorn they were sharing, or that she felt shivers down her spine when he leaned close to whisper in her ear during the movie. It wasn't his fault, but by the time the final credits rolled up on the screen, every nerve ending in her body was tingling with awareness.

And he seemed completely unaffected by their nearness. Of course he would be—he had dated a lot of women, beautiful and sophisticated women.

Which made her again wonder: What was he doing with her?

And what had happened to the guy who was reputed to go out with a different woman every night?

Because the man she was slowly getting to know didn't bear any resemblance to the Casanova he was reputed to be. Or maybe it was simply that he wasn't interested in anything other than friendship with her.

And that was okay, because she enjoyed being with him and talking to him and maybe, as they spent more time together, she would gradually stop acting like a silly schoolgirl with a crush on the captain of the football team.

Except that every time he touched her—a casual touch of his hand to her arm or an accidental brush of his shoulder against hers—she couldn't help thinking about the not-so-casual or accidental full-body contact that had occurred at Ashley and Trevor's engagement party.

Just the memory of the kiss they'd shared had enough power to steam her glasses, even when she wasn't wearing them.

After the movie, they went for pizza.

While they waited for their medium deep dish with hot sausage and hot peppers, they chatted casually about current events. While they ate, the conversation veered to work topics, and Megan asked him, "When you were growing up, was it always your plan to work at Richmond Pharmaceuticals?"

Gage shook his head. "First I wanted to be a fire-fighter, and then a baseball player...or maybe it was a baseball player then a firefighter."

She smiled. "Seven-year-olds are so indecisive."

"I was eight," he told her.

"And when you got a little older?"

He thought about the question, about the career options he'd considered through the years. There had been several, though none that he'd considered too seriously—aside from the microbrewery his friend Brian wanted them to start in college, when beer was very serious business to them. And he knew that he'd never thought too long or too hard about anything else because Richmond Pharmaceuticals had always been there.

The insight made him uneasy, but he responded casually to her question. "When I got a little older, I decided I would rather be a doctor or a rock musician."

"A doctor or a rock musician?"

"It was a tough call—help sick people or get lots of girls?"

"And somehow you manage to do both while working at R.P."

His smile was wry. "So the rumor goes."

"Does it bother you—being the subject of company gossip?"

"It didn't used to," he admitted. "Or maybe I was just unaware of it before. But recently it seems to have become an impediment to my career advancement."

"How so?"

"I had a conversation with my father recently," he admitted. "And he told me that my inability to commit to a relationship has given some members of the board cause to question my maturity and commitment."

He didn't specifically mention Dean Garrison's retirement because an official announcement hadn't yet been made—and because he realized, perhaps belatedly, that Megan might very well be his competition for the job.

"So long as you do your job well—and no one could argue against that—your personal life should be irrelevant," she said.

"I agree," he said. "But there are others who don't, and their opinions carry a lot of weight."

"How are you supposed to counter that?" she wondered.

"Show them that I can make a commitment." It was something he'd been thinking about since his conversation with his father and a decision that he hadn't made lightly.

"You're going to get married to impress the board of directors?"

"I have no intention of letting things go that far," he assured her. "I wasn't thinking of exchanging wedding vows but of getting engaged. At least temporarily."

"I don't think you can rent a fiancée as easily as a tuxedo," she cautioned.

"You're right, of course. But I was hoping, of all the women I've dated, one of them might be willing to do me a favor."

"That's quite a favor."

"I know," he agreed. "And even if I knew someone who was willing, the truth is, none of the women I've dated in the past is the type of woman I would settle down with."

"What does that say about the type of women you've dated?"

"None except one," he clarified.

She wiped her fingers on a paper napkin, then dropped it on her plate. "It still seems a little drastic to me," she warned.

"Desperate times call for desperate measures."

"Then I'll wish you luck."

He appreciated the sentiment, but he didn't need luck.

What he needed was to figure out a way to convince Megan to go along with his plan.

One of the reasons Paige went into her office on Saturdays was for the quiet. With the answering service handling all of the calls and most of the other lawyers and support staff away, she was able to focus on her work and catch up on anything that had slid during the week while she was busy with court appearances and settlement conferences and client meetings.

In each successive year since she'd started at Wainwright, Witmer & Wynne, she'd been given more clients and greater responsibilities. She enjoyed the work and believed she was providing an important service to her clients, many of whom were too emotionally distraught by the breakdown of their marriages to think clearly about their rights and entitlements. But the side effect of her professional success was personal disillusionment with respect to marital relationships.

This realization was weighing heavily on her mind as she drove out of the parking lot beside her building and spotted Trevor Byden walking down the street. Going to work, she assumed, since her cousin's fiancé's office was a few blocks north of her own.

But then she saw him stop to talk to a woman who had come from the other direction, and take the grocery bags she carried. The woman smiled and rose up to kiss him—full on the lips.

The honk of a horn alerted Paige to the fact that she was stopped at a green light. She tore her gaze away from the disturbing scene and pulled through the intersection. As she merged with the traffic on the highway, she began to doubt what she had seen.

Maybe it hadn't been Trevor.

It *couldn't* have been Trevor.

Because Trevor was engaged to Ashley and she trusted that he was in love with and faithful to her cousin.

Still, she thought about what she'd seen the entire way home, and considered whether or not to mention it to Ashley.

But what could she say?

"I saw a man who I thought was Trevor kissing another woman?"

Because the truth was, she'd caught a glimpse of his profile, and the sense of recognition combined with the proximity to his office had made her think he was her cousin's fiancé.

She wasn't 100 percent certain the man was Trevor and she couldn't tell Ashley it was, not without proof.

And she didn't want any proof. She wanted to believe Trevor was truly devoted to Ashley.

But as a family-law attorney, she'd dealt with far too many cheating spouses. Whether infidelity was the cause or effect of the marriage breakdown wasn't her judgment to make, she only knew that, far too often, there was a third party involved. And she was determined to ensure that Ashley not end up an unhappy statistic.

If it wasn't Trevor that she'd seen, then her cousin's fiancé had nothing to worry about. If it was Trevor—

No, Paige refused to acknowledge the possibility. She wanted to believe that her cousin's fiancé was one of the good guys, because she needed to believe that there were at least some of them left in the world.

Over the next few weeks, Megan and Gage spent a lot of time together. Most of it at the lab, as the clinical trial for Fedentropin finally got under way and they both put in a lot of overtime hours, but they began to hang out after work, as well, frequently going somewhere to grab a bite to eat or, if they'd ordered in at the lab, just for a drink to chat and unwind. It was never anything formal or fancy—certainly nothing that she would say qualified as a date—but she believed they were becoming friends.

So Gage's invitation to a barbecue at his parents' house didn't seem any more significant than any other meal and more shared conversation. Until she made the mistake of mentioning it to Ashley and Paige at one of their scheduled Friday night get-togethers.

It was Paige's night to cook, which meant actual home cooking. When it was Ashley's turn, they usually ate something that advertised "from freezer to oven to table" on the box, while Megan generally opted for pizza or Chinese or something else that could be delivered.

Paige was putting the finishing touches on her lasagna when Megan told them of her plans for the following night.

"He's taking you home to meet his parents," Ashley said, and while the statement wasn't inaccurate, there was something in the way she said it that made Megan think the words were all in capital letters and flashing lights.

"He invited me to a barbecue at their house," Megan clarified. "It's not a big deal. His brother's family will be there, too."

"The extended family," Paige said, in the same capital letters, flashing lights tone.

"It's not a big deal," Megan said again.

"Who are you trying to convince?"

"Gage *said* it wasn't a big deal."

"Because he didn't want you to get all freaked out about it," Ashley guessed.

"Or maybe because it's really *not* a big deal."

"Are you that oblivious?" Paige asked her.

Megan frowned. "Oblivious to what?"

Ashley shook her head. "How long have you been dating now?"

"We're not dating."

Paige sprinkled grated cheese on top of the sauce. "You've been going out together after work at least two or three times a week. What would you call it?"

"Going out with a coworker after work," Megan insisted stubbornly.

"But when that coworker is a sexy, single guy whose kisses pack enough heat to melt the polar ice caps, it's called dating."

"I might have to agree with you if I'd been getting any of those kisses."

Now it was Ashley's turn to frown. "You haven't?"

Megan shook her head.

"All of those nights you've spent together?" Paige pressed.

"Nada."

"What is wrong with that man?"

"Nothing's wrong with him—he just doesn't see me as anything more than a friend. Which is why I'm certain this dinner at his parents' isn't a big deal."

"He hasn't kissed you once?" Paige asked incredulously, not able to get past that fact.

"Not since Ashley and Trevor's engagement party."

"That does put a different spin on things," her cousin mused.

"Maybe he's just taking it slow," Ashley suggested.

"Or maybe he just wants to be friends," Megan said again, still unwilling to let herself hope they could be anything more.

* * *

It was a Friday night and instead of being out on a date or watching a game with some friends, Gage was surrounded by females. While he generally appreciated women of all shapes and sizes, he felt decidedly out of his element and outnumbered with his four nieces.

It was only supposed to be for a few hours, while Craig was at a late dinner meeting because Tess was away on a two-day business trip. After the first hour, Gage was at his wits' end because Gracie hadn't wanted to stop chatting online to come to the table for dinner, Eryn and Allie were grumbling because he wouldn't take them to the movie theater to catch a show with their friends, and Lucy had fallen off of the bathroom counter after climbing up to try and catch a particularly nasty-looking spider.

So when the pizza box was empty and the plates and cups loaded into the dishwasher, he decided to entertain them the only way he knew how: he taught them to play Texas Hold 'em.

He emptied the change out of the cup holder in his car and divvied it up so they had coins to wager with and he spent the next hour and a half teaching them the intricacies of this particular variation of seven-card stud. Lucy had just raked in the jackpot when her father finally walked in the door.

"Daddy, Daddy. I won!"

Craig's eyes glinted with amusement as he glanced around the table, noting the drinks and snacks and his four daughters in their pajamas.

"How much?" he asked Lucy.

She beamed as she finished counting. "A dollar thirty-two."

"Big stakes." He looked at his brother. "I hope you didn't hide the beer and cigars on my account."

Gage shook his head. "Turns out your girls prefer gin, and Gracie took one puff of a Cuban and turned green."

"I did not," Gracie said, then frowned. "A Cuban what?"

Craig chuckled. "Never mind. Go brush your teeth and get into bed."

Gage gladly tidied up the cards and snacks while his brother handled the bedtime routine.

When Craig came back downstairs, he disappeared into the kitchen for a moment then came out with two bottles of beer.

Gage took the one offered to him and studied the Millhouse Brew Co. label for a moment before he twisted off the cap. Millhouse was the company his friend, Brian, had been trying to convince Gage to invest in with him. But he'd declined, because he was a Richmond, and Richmonds made pharmaceuticals, not beer.

He lifted the bottle and took a long swallow, and had to admit that it was really good beer.

Craig propped his feet up on the coffee table. "Well, you survived," he said to his brother.

"Barely." Gage tipped the bottle to his lips again. "Don't they drive you insane?"

"Every day." His brother grinned. "And I couldn't imagine my life without them."

Gage knew it was true, but still, he wondered. "Did you ever worry—when Tess got pregnant, I mean—did you ever worry that you might not be able to stick it out?"

"Every day," Craig said again. "I guess that's not surprising, considering what we went through with Charlene."

Gage nodded, acknowledging the complete lack of maternal instincts possessed by the woman who had given birth to them.

"And then, the very first time I held Gracie in my

arms, I stopped worrying. Because I *knew* that nothing could ever matter more to me than my family, and nothing could ever make me leave them."

"Like Dad," Gage said. "He stuck with us even when she made his life hell."

"Do you remember that? You were hardly more than a baby."

"I don't remember a lot," he admitted. "But I've heard enough stories through the years to put the rest of the pieces together."

"Why are we talking about this now?"

"I guess I was just wondering if it's some kind of genetic defect that made Charlene incapable of really loving someone."

"And wondering if you inherited that genetic defect," his brother guessed.

"I'm thirty-two years old and I've never been in love," Gage admitted.

"What about Beth?"

He scowled at the reference to his ex or maybe he was scowling at his own naïveté in ever believing that he'd been in love with her. "Beth was a leech masquerading as a human being."

"That's a pretty harsh assessment."

"But not untrue."

"No," his brother agreed. "But you loved her, anyway, didn't you?"

"I think I was more in love with the idea of being in love," Gage admitted. "You and Tess had recently married, and I thought—for a while anyway—that I wanted what you had with her."

What he'd got, instead, was a girlfriend who expected unrestricted access to his bank to bail out the sister who kept falling into debt to her drug dealer.

He'd let himself be suckered in three times before he'd put Beth's sister in rehab and walked away from the whole mess, but not before the experience confirmed the lesson Charlene had taught him—that love of money was stronger than the affection anyone claimed to have for him.

"So why are you thinking about this now?" Craig asked him.

Gage frowned at the question, shrugged.

"Because I don't think you're really concerned that you've never been in love," his brother said. "I think you're concerned that you might now be falling."

"What? Are you kidding? No." He shook his head firmly. "No way."

His brother chuckled. "What was it Shakespeare said about protesting too much?"

"I was never a big fan of Shakespeare."

"Which is hardly the point."

"You were making a point?"

Craig shrugged. "You're the one who's bringing Megan to meet the family tomorrow night."

"Only because Mom badgered me into it."

"A piece of advice," Craig said. "Don't tell that to your girlfriend."

Gage suspected that Megan wouldn't accept that label so easily, but that was something he would worry about later.

As for worrying that he could fall in love—he wasn't, because he knew it would never happen. He wouldn't let it. Not again. And certainly not with Megan Roarke.

Chapter Eight

Megan had seemed so pleased the first time Gage took her flowers that he couldn't resist stopping at the florist again. This time it was a pot of sunny daffodils that snagged his attention—and earned him her sunny smile.

"I love daffodils," she admitted.

"That's what you said about the tulips."

She smiled. "They're both spring flowers, and that's always been my favorite season. A time of reawakening and renewal, when everything is fresh and anything seems possible."

"I like summer—backyard barbecues and baseball games. Cold beer and…" he trailed off, cleared his throat.

"Hot women in skimpy bikinis?" she guessed.

He grinned, acknowledging that he'd been caught. "I think I'd like to see you in a skimpy bikini."

"I doubt that," she said. "But thank you."

"For picturing you in a skimpy bikini?"

She blushed. "For the flowers."

"I have something else for you," he said, and handed her a letter-size envelope.

"What's this?"

"A standard form 'Notice of Disclosure of Personal Relationship with Trial Candidate,'" he explained. "After you've filled it out, your sister can come in to the clinic for the preliminary bloodwork so we can get her on the standby list."

"But she's not even twenty-nine. She doesn't fit the criteria for the study."

"We do sometimes extend the criteria," he reminded her. "So why didn't you ask if we could extend it for Ashley?"

"I thought about it," she admitted. "And I might have, if we'd had a shortage of candidates.

"The fact that we didn't further convinced me that the drug is desperately needed, and I'm keeping my fingers crossed that the test results prove successful so it can be made available to all of the women who didn't fit within the original group."

"We've had a couple of dropouts already," he noted.

The first woman had reluctantly withdrawn from the study because her husband's job was forcing them to move halfway across the country, making it impossible for her to come in for the required follow-up testing. The second woman had happily dropped out of the group when she realized she'd conceived within a few days of starting the protocol. He knew the woman's pregnancy was more likely a coincidence than a result of the drug, but it was a happy result nonetheless.

"How did you know about Ashley?" she finally asked him.

"There were clues. Your dedication to the research,

your focus on the trial, your sister's illness that you explained away as 'a female thing.' Are you really surprised that I was able to connect the dots?"

She shook her head. "Not surprised that you could, but that you would bother to do so. And grateful. Very grateful."

"We all have our own reasons for doing what we do," he told her. "You started the Fedentropin project for your sister, she should have the chance to benefit from it."

"Thank you," she said again, and rose on her toes to kiss his cheek.

It was a quick touch of her lips to his skin, nothing more than a fleeting brush, really. But when her gaze met his, the air was suddenly charged with an awareness that seemed to crackle between them like static electricity.

Megan took an instinctive step back.

Gage stepped closer, breaching the distance she'd deliberately put between them, so that she had to tip her chin up to maintain eye contact. But she didn't retreat any farther.

Her eyes widened as he lowered his head toward hers. This time she could have no doubt about his intention, and he watched as the violet depths of those fabulous eyes darkened as awareness took over... deepened as awareness gave way to desire.

He touched his mouth to hers gently at first, testing. But when her lips softened, parted, the response was like a jolt of electricity through his system, setting every nerve ending in his body on fire.

He forgot to be gentle, careful, and simply devoured her.

He dragged her against him, held her tight. She didn't resist but lifted her arms to link them behind his neck, her hands sliding through his hair, the touch of her fingertips against his scalp incredibly erotic.

The first time he'd kissed her, he'd been swept away by the intensity of her passionate response. This time, he'd thought he was prepared, but there was something about her transformation from shy, unassuming scientist to sexy, wanton woman that went straight to his blood.

Her lips parted, their sighs mingled, their tongues tangled. She pressed herself closer, her breasts crushing against his chest, her hips aligned with his, and he knew there was no way she could mistake the erection pushing against his zipper for anything other than what it was. Just as he knew that if she kept wriggling against him, they were never going to get out of her kitchen.

With extreme reluctance, he eased his lips from hers.

"I've tried not to do that," he admitted, when he'd finally caught his breath again.

"Why?"

"Because I didn't want the attraction between us to become a distraction."

"A distraction?" She seemed baffled by the thought.

And if his parents weren't expecting them, he might be tempted to take her back to his place and show her how completely she distracted him. But as much as he enjoyed spending time with Megan, taking their involvement to the next level would invariably ruin all of his plans.

He wanted a fake fiancée, not a real relationship, and so long as he remembered that, everything would work out just fine.

Despite all of Ashley's and Paige's warnings to the contrary, dinner with Gage's family wasn't in the scope of capital letters and flashing lights.

His parents were gracious and welcoming, which

she attributed partly to the fact that they were genuinely nice people and partly to the fact that they'd undoubtedly met a lot of Gage's female "friends" over the years. And though her friendship with their younger son was truly of the platonic variety—two sizzling kisses notwithstanding—they seemed genuinely pleased that she'd accepted the invitation to dinner.

Gage's brother, she already knew, of course. And she'd met his wife a couple of times at company functions, but it was Craig and Tess's four daughters who truly captivated her attention through the meal.

She'd grown up with a sister and, later on, with Paige, too, but she didn't ever remember family meals being such a cacophony of conversations. Everyone seemed to be talking at once and about different things, and though Megan didn't quite know what to say to anyone, she enjoyed trying to follow the various discussions around her.

"I told you it was chaos," Gage said, leaning close to whisper in her ear as his mother served up the trifle she'd made for dessert.

"It is that. But in a good way," she said. And she meant it.

His family had been truly wonderful, accepting her presence at the table without question. At least until she got up to help Tess clear the dishes away.

"How long have you and Gage been dating now?" his sister-in-law asked as she loaded plates into the dishwasher.

Gage, having followed them into the kitchen, didn't seem nearly as surprised by the inquiry as Megan was.

"It's been a couple of months now, hasn't it, sweetheart?" he responded to the question, sliding an arm across her shoulders.

Sweetheart?

Megan didn't know what was going on or why he wanted his family to believe they were together, but she decided to play along. For now.

"Has it been that long already?" she asked, the gentle tone in contrast to the icy glare she shot in his direction.

"Hard to believe, isn't it?" he drew her closer to his side, tried not to wince at the sharp elbow she discreetly jabbed into his ribs.

Tess's gaze slid from one to the other, but if she had any suspicions that things weren't quite as they appeared, she kept them to herself.

Megan turned on Gage as soon as he got in the car to drive her home at the end of the evening. "What was *that* about?"

To his credit, he didn't pretend not to know what she was talking about. "My dad made certain assumptions, based on the fact that we've been spending a lot of time together recently, and he seemed so pleased by the idea we were dating that I chose not to correct his assumption."

"And you didn't think to warn me?" she asked incredulously.

"I knew if I did, you'd refuse to come to dinner."

"You set me up."

He didn't deny it.

She shook her head, torn between anger and frustration and confusion. "But why would you want them to think that we're together?"

"Because I've been thinking about how to convince my dad that I'm not the irresponsible playboy everyone believes me to be, and it seemed obvious that you would make the perfect fiancée."

Fiancée? She felt a jolt of surprised pleasure at the

idea of wearing Gage's ring, of being with him forever. And then she remembered that he was only looking for a temporary fiancée, and reminded herself that he wasn't really interested in her except as a player in his game.

She shook her head. "Uh-uh. No way."

"Definitely you," he said. "You're the perfect choice."

"And why is that?" she challenged, already sure she knew the answer.

"Because you're the complete opposite of every other woman I've ever dated."

Yeah, it was just as she'd thought, but his confirmation still made her heart sink. "'Opposite' as in *not* glamorous, *not* sexy, *not* gorgeous, you mean?"

He winced. "No, that's not what I meant."

"It doesn't matter," she said, but it was a lie.

Though she was used to being overlooked—growing up with a sister as beautiful as Ashley, it was something she'd grown accustomed to early on—she'd thought he was different. She'd thought he saw who she was beneath the surface, and this acknowledgment that she was lacking in comparison to his usual companions stung.

What hurt even more was the realization that she'd once again let herself be fooled into believing that an attractive man might be interested in her, only to find out that he was just interested in what she could do for him.

"It doesn't matter," she said again. "Because there is no way I'm going to go along with such a ridiculous plan."

"It's not ridiculous."

"You said it yourself—I'm the opposite of every woman you've ever dated. Which is exactly why no one would believe it," she told him.

"My family believes it," he reminded her.

"Only because you deliberately misled them."

And she was furious that he'd done so—and frustrated that she hadn't realized what he was doing. She'd suspected that he had ulterior motives for being with her, but she'd been so happy being with him that she didn't bother to question his reasons.

"Remember my sister's engagement party? You were supposed to be my date, but that didn't stop my cousin from hitting on you."

"When I think about your sister's engagement party, that's not what I remember," he said, his gaze dropping deliberately to her mouth.

She wasn't going to succumb to such a blatant effort to distract her. She refused to think about that kiss.

Okay, maybe she'd dreamed about it—frequently and in great detail. And maybe those dreams sometimes went beyond a kiss. But while she couldn't control her subconscious mind while she was sleeping, she refused to let her wayward fantasies take hold while she was awake.

"Besides," Gage continued. "My parents already think we're together."

"And whose fault is that?" she grumbled.

"Why is it necessary to assign blame?" he asked mildly.

She shook her head. "I still can't believe they would believe you could be interested in me."

"You're a beautiful, intelligent woman, Meg."

She couldn't resist rolling her eyes at that, certain he was only flattering her in the hopes of persuading her to go along with his plan. Because she knew that letting her hair down and wearing contact lenses were hardly enough to transform her from science geek to desirable woman.

"You are," he insisted. "And my parents like you."

"So?"

"They've never liked any of the women I've dated before."

"Then find someone they will like—someone other than me."

"My mom will be extremely disappointed to learn that our relationship is over almost before it began."

"There is no relationship," she said firmly.

"I'm only asking for a six-month engagement," he said, obviously having given the matter some thought.

She ignored him.

"A six-month engagement, especially to someone who is completely unlike any other woman I've ever dated, will convince everyone that I've mended my ways. After the six months, you can dump me and break my heart."

"Then your parents would really like me."

"They'll accept that I did something to screw up the best relationship I ever had," he told her. "It's something of a pattern with me."

"Why is that?" she couldn't help but ask.

He lifted a shoulder. "If I wanted to be psychoanalyzed, I'd go to a shrink."

But the casual gesture was at odds with the shadows she saw in his eyes.

"A fiancée would be expected to know your dating history," she prompted.

"There's nothing to know," he insisted. "Except that I've never had a relationship that was serious or long-term."

"Never?"

"Not in a very long time," he amended.

"She must have hurt you deeply," Megan said.

He shrugged again. "Or maybe I'm just a commitment phobe," he said, obviously unwilling to share any details. "But, of course, everything changed when I met you. For the first time in my life, I could not just imagine but look forward to spending the rest of my life with one woman."

It took her a moment, but she realized he was merely explaining the rationale that he would give to anyone else who asked why he wanted to marry Megan—if she agreed to go along with his engagement scam.

Which, of course, she wouldn't.

She wouldn't let herself be sucked into his plan, no matter how much she wanted to be with him.

For three days, Megan pushed all thoughts of Gage's proposal from her mind—or tried to. Let him find some other willing woman if he was determined to see this crazy scheme through. Because she had no doubt that he would. Gage Richmond wasn't a man who was ever without a woman if he wanted one.

Okay, so maybe it had given her ego a little boost— albeit a temporary one—that this time he'd wanted *her*. Then reality had come crashing back when she realized his interest was solely for the purpose of a role-playing exercise. And he was so oblivious to everything except his own goals that he didn't even realize how insulting his offer was.

Slamming the car door, she started up the walk to her house. Ashley was already home, and she considered venting some of her frustration to her, but her sister had seemed more than a little preoccupied recently—no doubt with preparations for the wedding—and Megan was reluctant to dump anything else on her.

Going into the kitchen, she filled the kettle with water and set it on the stove to boil. There was a stack of mail on the counter, and she thumbed through it. Credit-card application. An offer for a free estimate on window replacement. A take-out menu for the local deli. Water bill. Telephone bill. And a thick square envelope with the logo of her old high school in the upper left-hand corner and her name and address neatly printed at the center.

She tore open the flap of that one. She thought it might be a request for financial support from the alumni association, but those usually came in a standard-size envelope with a preprinted label. This one had a textured card inside, embossed with elegant gold script urging her to "Remember When…"

It was an invitation to celebrate the tenth anniversary of her graduation and the one hundredth year of the school.

Cream-colored vellum and gold text?

If the reunion committee wanted to evoke memories of high school, the invitations should have been scribbled with a Bic pen on a sheet of lined paper torn out of a spiral-bound notebook. And even then Megan wouldn't go. She had no intention of reliving the nightmare that had been high school.

She'd been twelve in her freshman year and by taking summer courses, she'd completed all of the requisite credits to graduate by the time she was fifteen. Her father had always been proud of her academic accomplishments, her mother had always worried that she did nothing but study, and they'd both encouraged her to take a break from school in the summer, to explore other interests.

Megan hadn't seen any point in taking a break and she didn't have any other interests. At least if she was busy reading and learning and studying, she had a reason for not doing normal teenage girl things like gossiping about boys and painting her toenails and staying up all night at slumber parties. And it was a better reason than the truth—that she was too much of an oddball to have many friends.

She stuffed the invitation back into the envelope and tossed it into the garbage.

If not for Ashley, Megan would have spent her childhood and teenage years completely alone. But her older sister was and always had been her best friend. It didn't seem to matter to Ashley that Megan would cut open her dolls to examine what was inside rather than dress them in pretty clothes, or that she'd opted to read about organic chemistry over Sweet Valley High.

There had always been a bond between them, the special connection that exists between sisters despite their differences. And when Paige came to live with them in her sophomore year, Megan had gained another rare ally in the halls of Hill Park High School.

The sound of footsteps on the stairs pulled Megan back to the present. She noted the yoga pants and t-shirt Ashley was wearing and said, "I thought you were going out tonight."

"Trevor had a client emergency and had to cancel our dinner plans."

"What kind of emergency does an accountant have to deal with?" She took two mugs out of the cupboard. "Did someone put a debit entry into the credit column?"

Her sister shrugged. "If it even was a real emergency."

Megan's smile slipped. "What do you mean?"

"I've been feeling tired and crampy and depressed and I think Trevor just didn't want to be with me tonight."

Megan knew she should bite her tongue, but she hated to see her sister uncomfortable and unhappy, and she knew Ashley was both.

"I wish you'd go back on the Pill," she said gently. "At least until after the wedding."

Ashley started to cry.

Megan rubbed a hand down her sister's arm. "It was just a suggestion."

"It was Trevor's suggestion, too," she admitted. "I

thought he wanted to have a baby as much I do, but he says he can't live with me like this.

"I think—" she drew in a breath "—I think there might not be a wedding."

Megan refused to believe it. She knew that Trevor loved Ashley, though she also knew that her sister's desire to have a child had put a strain on their relationship.

"Of course there will be a wedding. And, as an early present, I have some good news," she said now, thinking her sister could use some. "Gage's father has cleared it so that you can be put on the standby list for the trial."

Ashley's eyes widened. "Really?"

"Once that's done, we can start you on the protocol, even if it has to be outside of the test group."

Ashley twisted the engagement ring on her finger. "How soon will that be?"

"Within a couple of months. Maybe sooner."

"Even that might be too late. Trevor might have given up on me by then."

"I can't imagine Trevor would give up on you without trying to work things out first."

"He *is* trying," Ashley said. "He thinks that I'm not, that I can't think about anything but having a baby."

"Is he wrong?" Megan asked gently, handing her sister a cup of tea.

"No." Ashley sighed as she cradled the cup between her palms. "I thought loving Trevor and having him love me would be enough, but it's not. I want a baby, and he's insistent that we continue to use protection until after the wedding."

Megan didn't say anything. Having never experienced the euphoria of being in love—or the heartbreak that sometimes followed—she felt distinctly unqualified to offer any sort of advice on the topic. On the other hand, disappointment and disillusionment were subjects on which she could write theses.

"Don't you understand, Meg? Don't you want to get married and have a family someday?"

"Sure," she agreed, although her dismal track record with men had stifled any dreams that might have moved in that direction. "Although right now I'd settle for a real date with someone who wants to be with me for me, without any ulterior motives."

Ashley seemed startled by her comment. "What does that mean?"

Megan shook her head, already regretting the words she'd spoken. "Nothing."

But her sister wasn't prepared to let it go. "Are you talking about Gage?"

"Funny you should ask," Megan muttered.

"What did he do?" Ashley demanded, automatically coming to her sister's defense.

"He told his parents that we're dating."

"You *are* dating."

"We're not, really," Megan insisted. "It's an illusion he's created. And do you know why he wanted me to meet his family? Because I'm the complete opposite of every other woman he's ever dated."

"He didn't use those actual words?"

"Those exact words," she assured her.

Ashley winced sympathetically.

"Apparently his reputation could be an impediment to his promotion within the company, and he actually proposed a mock engagement to convince the world that he's changed his ways."

Megan thumped her sister on the back when she started to choke on her tea.

"Does this mock engagement include a real diamond?" Ashley asked, when she could speak again.

Megan had to laugh. "We didn't get that far in the negotiations."

"Why not?"

"Because I told him no way, no how would I go along with his scheme."

"I think you should reconsider."

Megan stared at her sister. "You're kidding."

Ashley shook her head. "Don't you see? You're in control here. This guy needs you."

"But I don't need him."

"But you want him," Ashley guessed.

Megan felt her cheeks flush.

The problem with having a sister who knew her so well was that Ashley knew when Megan was lying—as she would be lying if she denied having certain X-rated fantasies about her boss's son.

"Do you remember how everyone looked at you differently at my engagement party because you were with Gage?"

Though Megan couldn't guess where her sister was going with this, she nodded.

"Imagine that same scene, but a lot bigger. Maybe a thousand people."

Megan shuddered at the thought. "You know I hate crowds."

"But you can block everyone else out, because you have Gage by your side and his ring on your finger."

"What are you talking about?"

"The Hill Park High School reunion."

"I am *not* going to the reunion."

"Why not?"

"For the same reason I never went to any social functions in high school. I was 'Roarke the Dork'—a certified geek and perennial outcast—and I have no desire to be reminded of that."

"You're not a geek anymore. And this is the perfect opportunity to show everyone the beautiful successful woman you are now."

"I appreciate the vote of confidence, but I'm still not going."

"Do you remember Tara Gallagher?"

"As if I could ever forget," she muttered.

The perky cheerleader was the complete opposite of Megan in every way and she'd been the bane of her existence during all of her days at Hill Park.

"Tara's head of the reunion committee."

"Which is just one more reason not to go, as if I didn't have enough reasons already."

Ashley shook her head. "You're not looking at the big picture. Forget all the nasty little things that Tara did to you in high school and imagine the look on her face when you walk into the room with the man recently voted one of America's one hundred most desirable bachelors."

"Did he really make the list again?"

"Moved up twelve spots from last year," Ashley confirmed. "Tara wouldn't be able to stand seeing him with you."

"Oh…that *is* tempting."

"And then there are all the pitiful jocks who scorned you because you were so much smarter than them."

Megan's little bubble burst. "Are you trying to convince me to go or not?"

"One thing you need to remember about men," Ashley told her. "They always want what they can't have."

Megan let herself consider the possibility for a minute, then shook her head. "If I went along with Gage's plan just so I have some spectacular arm candy for the reunion, then I'd be using him in the same way he's trying to use me."

"Think of it as a win-win situation," Ashley said.

Megan couldn't deny that she was tempted. But if she let herself get caught up in Gage's plan, she might get caught up in Gage, too—and end up with her heart broken.

And that was a chance she wasn't willing to take.

Chapter Nine

Gage accepted that he might have pushed Megan too far and too fast, but time was slipping away. Even more so since that damned list had been printed again. Sure he'd got a kick out of being named one of the country's most desirable bachelors when he'd first made the list four years earlier, but his continued rise on the list only seemed to underline his father's concerns. If he was going to ensure that it was his name stenciled on the door of the V.P. office when Dean Garrison retired, he needed to set his plan in motion fast.

He considered, briefly, the possibility of finding another woman to play the role of his fiancée, but he really couldn't think of anyone else he would want to spend six months of his life with. It was a sad commentary on the character of the women he'd previously dated—and his own taste—that he couldn't imagine a relationship lasting any longer than six weeks. Megan was the only woman he could imagine being with for such an extended period of time without being bored to death.

In fact, the more time he spent with Megan, the more fascinated he was by her. She was smart and fun, compassionate and witty. They never seemed to run out of things to talk about and even when they weren't talking, the silence was never awkward or uncomfortable.

Okay, the attraction was a complication that he hadn't anticipated, and it did worry him a little. A fake engagement would only succeed if they both remembered that it was fake, and he knew that wouldn't be easy when the attraction between them was so real. But he was sure he could handle it. He only had to remember what was at stake: the V.P. office.

And because the stakes were so high, he couldn't give up.

So when he and Megan were the last ones in the lab Thursday night, he said, "You know I never seriously thought about marriage before my father started in on me about why I haven't been moving up in the company."

"And you're seriously thinking about marriage now?" she challenged.

"No," he admitted. "But I've started thinking about why I never wanted to settle down, and I realized that it's probably because I don't like to fail."

"No one likes to fail," she said reasonably.

"That's why I've never dated anyone for more than a few months—because I don't want to set up any expectations."

"And you're telling me…why?"

"Because, as you previously noted, a fiancée would be expected to know this stuff."

"I'm *not* your fiancée."

"I know, but I'm working on it."

"I'm flattered," she said, in a tone that warned him she was anything but.

"If you want flowers and candlelight, I can do that."

Megan shook her head. "It's not the delivery of the proposal that I have a problem with but the proposal itself."

"Why?"

"Because an engagement—even a fake one—would be too much of a complication at this point in my life."

"It doesn't have to be complicated," he promised.

"You don't understand," she told him. "If I agreed to this, if my mother got so much as a whiff of a proposal, she'd be booking the church."

Despite her adamant tone, the *if* gave Gage hope. Until then, he'd been certain he was fighting a losing battle in trying to convince Megan to go along with his plan.

So he considered his response carefully, all too aware of the narrow edge between persuasive and pushy as he attempted to negotiate it. He wasn't sure why it was so important to him to play out the charade with Megan, only that it was.

"We'll just explain that we want a long engagement," he told her.

"*We* don't want *any* engagement," she said, but he thought she sounded more wistful than exasperated.

"I'll let you pick the ring. Whatever you want—the sky's the limit."

She folded her arms across her chest, and he tried—really tried—not to look at her breasts. Yeah, they were modest, but when they'd been pressed against his chest, he'd known without a doubt that they were real.

"Do you really think you can bribe me with diamonds?" she challenged.

"No," he admitted, forcing his attention back to their conversation and accepting the fact as further proof that

Megan wasn't like any other woman he'd ever dated. Most women would have jumped at his offer, if only to see how much of his inheritance he was willing to spend on a ring.

"So what can I bribe you with?" he asked, still hoping he might find a way to secure her cooperation.

She opened her mouth, then closed it again without saying a word.

"Now is not the time to start censoring your thoughts. Just tell me."

"There's nothing you have that I want."

But the way her cheeks flushed suggested she wasn't being entirely honest in her response.

"Except?" he prompted.

The color in her cheeks deepened. "Your experience and reputation," she finally admitted.

"Excuse me?"

She shrugged. "Since we've been working together on this trial, rumors—apparently not as unfounded as I previously believed—have been circulating that we're...involved. And since then, well, people have been looking at me differently."

He frowned. "What people?"

The color in her cheeks deepened. "Men."

"Looking at you differently how?" he demanded.

"As if...maybe...they missed something before." She dropped her gaze. "As if...maybe...they might be interested."

He wasn't sure why her statement annoyed him, only that it did. "What does that have to do with my proposal?"

"Well, it occurred to me—" she still refused to look at him "—that if I was engaged to you, and if I was the one who dumped you at the end, it might increase my appeal. Popularity by association."

He couldn't believe what she was saying. But obviously *she* believed it, and he was seriously annoyed to realize that she could think so little of herself.

"Meg, any guy who only wants you because someone else wanted you is an idiot."

Finally she looked up at him. "*You* only want me because you think your parents approve of me."

It was true, but not the whole truth. The truth was, he had a lot of reasons for wanting her to play the part of his fiancée—some of which he wasn't yet ready to explore too deeply.

"Actually, I could probably find someone else to go along with my plan," he told her. "But if I have to fake an engagement for six months, I thought it should be to someone I enjoy being with, someone who can carry on an intelligent conversation, someone—" his lips curved "—who tells me when I'm being an idiot."

She smiled, too. "That I can do."

He looked at her hopefully.

She sighed. "Okay. I'll consider your proposition… on one condition."

He had expected a little more resistance, and a lot more conditions, so he didn't hesitate. "Name it."

"You have to be faithful."

He scowled, equal parts annoyed and offended. "As if I'd be with another woman while my ring is on your finger."

"How long has it been since you've had sex?"

The blunt question shocked him—as did the realization that she expected him to answer it. Instead, he asked a question of his own. "What does *that* have to do with anything?"

"You said it's been several months since you've dated anyone," she reminded him. "I assumed, though I know it's not necessarily true, that means it's been several months since you've had sex."

"So?"

"To go six more months seems like it's asking a lot of a man like you."

"Now who's making generalizations?" he grumbled.

"You don't think it will be a hardship?" she challenged.

"Not one I can't handle," he said, and prayed it was true. Not that he wanted any woman but her—and that would be the biggest challenge, keeping his hands off of the woman who was supposedly his fiancée.

"What if there was another option?"

His gaze narrowed as he picked up a tray of samples. "What other option?"

"My sexual experience is decidedly lacking," she explained. "But if even half of the rumors I've heard are true, yours is not."

He put the tray in the freezer before the implication of her statement sank in, and he scowled at her, all too aware that he was as aroused as he was infuriated. "You've got to be joking."

She flinched at the harshness of his response and turned away, but not before he saw the glitter of tears she tried to hide. He'd been shocked by her proposition and he'd reacted instinctively, but he hadn't intended to hurt her, and he felt like dirt, knowing that he had.

"Fine. Forget I said anything. I thought—the way you kissed me—" She shook her head. "I guess it was just another one of those games I have no experience with. Well, you could have just said you didn't want me and saved us both the embarrassment of my proposal."

Could she really think that? Believe that?

"Meg." He put his hands on her shoulders, winced when she jerked away. "It wasn't a game."

She faced him again, her eyes shining with as much fury as hurt. "Then what was it?"

He reached up to tuck a strand of hair behind her cheek.

She stilled, every muscle in her body tensing, but didn't pull away.

"Impulse," he admitted softly. "Desire. Need."

Her eyes clouded with confusion.

And the urge to take her in his arms and kiss away the hurt he'd inadvertently caused was almost more than he could resist. "Do you really think I could kiss you like that and not want a hell of a lot more?"

"I don't know," she admitted.

He heard the vulnerability in her words, saw it in her eyes, and acknowledged that she had a lot to learn. As tempted as he was to teach her about the games men and women played, he knew that would only hurt her in the end, and that was a risk he wouldn't take. But she was hurting now and that, at least, was something he could fix.

"Lesson number one," he said. "Men are simple creatures. We want what we want and we can't fake arousal."

"You're saying that you *are* attracted to me?"

He couldn't lie to her, not about this, not when his response obviously mattered so much to her. "Yes, I'm attracted to you."

Her brow furrowed. "Then why are you so opposed to this?"

"Because I like you."

The furrow deepened. "Excuse me?"

He scrubbed a hand though his hair. "Okay. I realize that doesn't make much sense."

"Are you saying that you usually have sex with women you don't like?"

"It's not that I don't like them. I wouldn't go out with

a woman I didn't enjoy being with. But there was rarely anything deeper than a certain elemental attraction, no real emotional involvement.

"Our relationship is already more complicated than that," he told her. "Not just because we work together, but because we're friends. Adding intimacy to the equation just makes everything more complicated."

She considered his explanation for a minute. "It could," she allowed. "If I had any expectations of our relationship continuing beyond the term of our fake engagement. But I don't want anything more from you than some basic male-female dating experience."

He frowned, not pleased to think that he was supposed to teach her the skills she would use to flirt with and seduce other men. Because even if that was what she believed she wanted, she had no idea how many piranhas were swimming in the dating pool, and how quickly her innocence would be devoured.

"Why now?" he asked. "Why me?"

"Because I'm too old to still be getting all nervous and tongue-tied every time a man shows the slightest hint of interest. And because you want me to go along with this engagement idea and it seems like a good way for us both to get something we want."

"I'm willing to do almost anything if you'll go along with this, but I'm not sure you understand what you're asking."

"Oh, for goodness' sake," she said. "I'm not offering myself as a virgin sacrifice on the altar of the almighty Gage Richmond. I've had sex before—just not very good sex."

Okay, so she did understand what she was asking—and he was beginning to understand that he was in big trouble. She might not be a virgin, but she was still innocent—far too innocent for him, and far too tempting.

"I'm flattered that you think sex with me would be different," he said drily.

"Your reputation precedes you."

"Which is exactly what got me into this dilemma in the first place," he reminded her.

She frowned, as if only now understanding the irony of her suggestion. "But if you want my help to get you out of it, I should get something in return."

She was right, of course, and since she seemed to know what she wanted, he would be a fool not to accept her offer. And if he had to have sex with her along the way, well, it would hardly be a sacrifice. In fact, considering how his body was already responding to the idea, it wouldn't be a sacrifice at all.

"Okay," he said. "Let's go get you a ring."

"Now?" Megan stared at him.

Gage shrugged. "Why not now?"

"Because…because…" She couldn't think why not, she could only think that she'd violated the age-old proverb that advocated "look before you leap." Now she was free-falling with no idea how long it would take before she hit bottom but certain that it would be with a great big *splat* when she did.

"Everyone already believes we've been dating for a while," he reminded her. "So it won't come as a complete surprise."

"Not to them," she muttered, as he took her hand and dragged her toward the door.

Megan followed, not certain if the flutters in her belly were caused by excitement or apprehension. Flutters that continued to intensify throughout the drive to the jewelry store while various questions raced through her mind: What had she gotten herself into? Was she really going to do this? Would anyone actually believe that Gage Richmond would ever want to marry her?

And—would he hold up his end of the bargain?

Her cheeks burned as she thought back to their conversation. She'd actually said that she wanted him to tutor her in the art of seduction and, even more surprising, he'd agreed. Not without reservations, but still he had agreed.

According to Paige, who knew a lot more about male-female dynamics than Megan, the current term was *friends with benefits*. And Megan trusted that so long as she remembered to focus on the *friends* part, she would get through the next six months with her heart intact.

"Most women are flushed with excitement when they walk into a jewelry store," Gage said, as they made their way down the sidewalk toward The Diamond Jubilee. "You look as if you're facing an execution."

"I feel like I'm going to throw up," she admitted.

He took an instinctive step back and she laughed.

"I'm not really going to do it," she promised. "It's just that when I get really nervous, my stomach tightens up."

"If anyone should be nervous, it should be me," Gage said. "This is definitely not a day I ever imagined would come."

"Ever?"

He shook his head decisively.

"Because then you would tumble from the national ranking of the country's most desirable bachelors?" she couldn't resist teasing.

"Actually, that might be a nice benefit of this engagement."

"Except that you're still a bachelor until marriage, and this engagement will be over long before next year's list."

"I can't believe you read that list."

"I don't. My sister does." She paused at the door, the knots in her stomach twisting.

"Take a deep breath, relax and remember it's not real," Gage advised. "That's what's getting me through."

He spoke nothing more than the truth, and yet she couldn't deny the pang of regret that echoed in her heart, the yearning for something more than a charade, for someone to truly love her.

But she knew that wasn't going to happen now, and it certainly wasn't going to happen with Gage, so she nodded and repeated the mantra inside her head as she stepped through the door he held open for her.

There were several other people in the store, mostly couples, she noted, which allowed them to browse the display cases uninterrupted while the sales staff assisted other customers.

Megan was overwhelmed by the selection. She'd never been one to stroll through jewelry stores, had never let herself dream. Now she wasn't just dreaming—she was actually going to walk out of the store as Gage Richmond's fiancée.

It's not real, she told herself again, willing the words to settle the flutters in her tummy and ignoring the disappointment that weighed heavily in her heart.

"Do you see anything you like?" Gage asked her.

She nodded and pointed to a pretty round-cut diamond solitaire set on a simple gold band.

Gage frowned. "You're kidding."

"You don't like it?"

"I don't think anyone would even see it on your finger."

The diamond was smaller than a lot of the others, but she didn't want something that would constantly draw attention to her. But even as the thought formed in her mind, she realized that was exactly what Gage did want.

"What about this one?" He gestured toward the center of the case and to a ring that was set apart from all the others not just by the set-up of the display but by its uniqueness and size.

Megan stared at the ring, at the cluster of diamonds so big and brilliant it was absolutely stunning, and shook her head. "I couldn't wear something like that."

"Sure you could."

She shook her head again.

"At least try it on, see how it looks."

"I like the small solitaire."

"The whole point in putting a ring on your finger is to show that I've made a commitment, which I would want to show in a big way."

"I like the solitaire," she insisted, all too aware that she sounded like a spoiled child. "And you said that I could pick the ring."

Gage sighed. "But if we want people to believe our engagement is real, the ring needs to be believable."

"I just think it's ridiculous to spend a fortune on something that is nothing more than a prop."

"I'm not worried about the money."

"You should be. You could probably buy a house for what that cluster of rocks will cost."

"Not a whole house," he denied. "But you might be able to make a good down payment."

"Then maybe I'll hock it when the engagement is over and pay off my mortgage."

"You can do whatever you want with it when our engagement is over," he agreed. "So long as you keep it on your finger until then."

In her head, Megan knew their engagement was only for the short-term. But in her heart, there was a tiny little piece that hoped she wouldn't ever have to take the showy ring off of her finger once Gage put it there.

Chapter Ten

Gage had considered making reservations at a fancy restaurant and having the waiter deliver the ring in Megan's dessert, but that seemed a little too staged. Besides which, he wasn't sure either of them was prepared for such immediate and public scrutiny of their engagement. Instead, he opted for a quiet, romantic dinner at home, setting the scene with flowers and wine, candlelight and music.

It wasn't until they were riding in the elevator up to his condo that he realized she had never been there before. And when he took her hand, he felt the tremble of her nerves.

Did she think he was taking her to his place so that he could jump her? Not that the thought hadn't crossed his mind more than once since she'd put sex on the bargaining table.

She'd called it "basic male-female dating experience" but they both knew she was talking about sex. And being a man, he couldn't seem to get the thought out of his mind. As he opened the door of his condo, he was wishing that he'd gone with the restaurant idea after all.

He hung her coat in the front closet and invited her to take a look around while he checked on dinner.

He was lighting the candles in the dining room when she made her way there.

"Wow," she said, obviously impressed.

"It seemed the kind of momentous occasion for which a man would make an effort," he said lightly. "Champagne?"

She nodded. "Please."

He popped the cork on the bottle of Pol Roger that had been chilling in a stainless-steel bucket and poured two glasses.

He handed one flute to Megan, then tapped the rim of his against hers. "Cheers."

She lifted her glass, sipped.

"Dinner is ready whenever you want to eat," he told her.

"You cooked?"

"Would you be impressed if I said I did?"

"I'm already impressed," she told him. "But I would wonder when you had the time."

"Nothing gets past you, does it?" He topped up her champagne. "Actually, I picked up takeout from The Silver Lotus and put it in the oven to keep it warm."

"I could eat." She gestured with her glass of champagne. "I should eat before I drink any more of this."

So Gage set the food out on the table and they ate spring rolls and mango chicken with tiger shrimp and jasmine rice. As they ate, they talked, and they drank more champagne, and gradually Megan began to relax.

It truly was the perfect setting for a romantic proposal,

she thought. Perfect, that is, if they had been a couple in love and looking forward to a future together. But for Megan, knowing that their future had a predetermined time limit, it was bittersweet.

She'd grown up believing that fairy tales were for princesses, and that she was destined to be a supporting character. But somehow, being with Gage made her feel like a princess. And while this interlude with him was nothing more than that, she would take it and the thrill of having her very own prince for as long as it lasted.

But for just a moment, she let herself imagine what it would be like to fall in love with someone like Gage, to be loved by someone like Gage, and she knew it would be a dream come true.

Then he got down on one knee beside her chair, with the ring box in his hand, and though she knew it wasn't real, she couldn't prevent her heart from fluttering in response to the old-fashioned romanticism. Which was precisely why she hadn't wanted this to happen.

"What are you doing?" she asked, unable to keep the panic from her voice.

He frowned. "Isn't it obvious?"

"This isn't necessary," she said. "Just give me the ring."

"But what if someone asks you how I proposed?"

She hadn't thought that far ahead, had believed it would be enough just to wear his ring on her finger, but she realized now that it was something she should have considered. "I'll make something up."

"This way you won't have to," he told her, and took her hand.

She knew he was right, and yet, it just felt…wrong.

And despite his determination to formally propose, his hesitation told her that he thought so, too.

"Megan…" He paused to clear his throat, probably of the words that were sticking there.

No matter that they each had their own reasons for agreeing to this arrangement, to actually propose would be a mockery of the special moment that every girl—even the geeky ones—dreamed of. And she couldn't let that happen.

"Yes," she said, giving him the answer he needed without waiting for the question neither of them wanted to hear him ask.

His relief was almost palpable as he took the ring out of the box and slid it on her finger. Then he exhaled audibly and rose to his feet.

She stared at the diamond cluster that somehow seemed even larger—and felt a lot heavier—on her hand. She swallowed. "I guess that makes it official."

"Not quite."

Now that the awkwardness of the big moment had passed, he seemed more relaxed, the familiar teasing glint replacing the uncertainty she'd seen in his eyes only a few minutes earlier.

"I can't imagine that you forgot anything," she said.

"I didn't." He took her hands and drew her up so that she was standing in front of him. "You did."

"I did?"

He nodded. "A truly appreciative woman would throw her arms around her fiancé and kiss him breathless."

It wasn't a challenge she would ordinarily have taken, but the three glasses of champagne had obviously impaired her judgment because she did exactly as he suggested.

Gage should have learned by now to expect the unexpected with Megan. But while he knew she would accept his challenge, he hadn't expected that she would wrap her arms around his neck and fasten her mouth to his in a kiss that actually did take his breath away.

Her lips were even softer than he remembered, and not nearly as tentative. She nibbled, and tugged gently with her teeth, then she slipped her tongue inside his mouth and began a slow, lazy exploration that had all of the blood in his head draining south.

And then she pressed against him, her breasts rubbing against his chest, her pelvis rocking against his, and desire shot through his system like flame-tipped arrows—fiery and dangerous.

He grabbed her hips and pulled her even closer. She moaned, not in protest but pleasure, and even as he took control of the kiss, plundering the sweet recesses of her mouth, he cursed her for starting something he knew he couldn't finish—not if he was going to look at his own reflection in the mirror in the morning.

After several more delicious, torturous minutes, he reluctantly eased his mouth from hers. But he continued to hold her, his chin resting on the top of her head, while he steadied his breathing and tried to slow the rush of blood through his veins.

"Apparently you have a handle on that kiss-me-breathless part."

"I'm a pretty quick study," she said, the words muffled against his chest.

She was that. She was also incredibly responsive and unexpectedly passionate and the soft, sexy noises she made in her throat when he was touching her nearly drove him to distraction.

So much so that, for the first time, he seriously began to question to wisdom of this engagement project. Because although they both knew it wasn't real, playing the part would mean spending a lot of time with her, and he knew he wouldn't be able to keep his hands off of her for very long.

Of course, she hadn't asked him to keep his hands off of her. In fact, she'd asked him *not* to keep his hands off of her. But he doubted that she wanted or expected to be horizontal and naked within minutes of his ring being put on her finger.

"I think it's probably time for me to take you home."

"I can take a cab," she said.

"Why would you want to do that?"

"Because we shared a whole bottle of champagne."

"I had one glass," he told her. "You drank the rest."

"Oh. Well. I guess that explains why my head is spinning." She looked up at him, smiled the shy little smile that never failed to tug at his heart. "I thought it was you. Being with you. Kissing you."

Yeah, she was definitely feeling the effects of the wine.

"I wasn't trying to get you drunk," he said, guilt and concern quickly overpowering any residual lust.

"I'm all right," she insisted. "And I'm not entirely sure it is the champagne, because I felt the same way after you kissed me the first time."

"You did?"

She nodded. "I've never felt so much from a kiss. Never wanted so much. You certainly know how to stir up a woman."

"I think those bubbles might have affected you more than you realize," he warned.

"I'm babbling, aren't I? I tend to do that when I've been drinking, which is why I usually don't drink much on dates. Not that I date much. Or didn't used to. And not that I'll be dating much now, seeing as we're supposed to be engaged.

"But when we break up, maybe I'll date more then. Ashley told me this engagement would be good for me, because men always want what they can't have." She tilted her head to look up at him. "Is that true?"

Those wide violet eyes tempted him beyond belief. Damn, he hated playing by the rules. But he had never— would never—take advantage of a woman who was obviously under the influence.

"I'd have to say, in this moment, it is entirely too true. And that is why I'm going to take you home now."

"I'm not ready to go home," she said, sliding her palms over his chest. "Not yet."

He snagged her wrists in his hands and prayed for the strength to endure the seduction of her innocence.

It was only the first day in what they had agreed would be a six-month engagement and he suspected that he would spend a lot of that time praying for the willpower to resist her.

When Megan followed the scent of fresh coffee into the kitchen the next morning, she found both Ashley and Paige waiting for her. She took a mug out of the cupboard and poured herself a cup.

It was Ashley who spotted the ring first.

"Oh. My. God."

"I told him it was too much," Megan said, when Paige snatched her hand for a closer inspection.

"It might not be your style," her cousin agreed. "But it's definitely an attention grabber."

"In a good way," Ashley hastened to add, when Megan made a face.

"Yeah, instead of putting an engagement announcement in the paper, I can just walk around town waving my hand."

"Speaking of announcements," Paige said, "when are you going to tell Gage's family?"

"He wants us to go over to his parents' place tonight, but I'm not sure I'm ready for that kind of scrutiny."

"Then you better get ready, because no one will believe the engagement is real if the happy couple doesn't show up together."

Megan sighed. "I know you're right."

"How do you think they'll take the news?" Ashley asked.

"I'm sure they'll be surprised, but Gage is confident they won't be displeased." She picked up a cinnamon bun from the plate at the center of the table and tore off a piece. "I, on the other hand, am feeling more than a little guilty, knowing that I'm deceiving these terrific people for no reason."

"You have a reason," Ashley reminded her. "To shake up your good-girl image."

"Maybe being a good girl isn't so bad."

"Trust me," Paige said. "It's a lot better being a little bad. Or being with a bad boy."

Megan shook her head. "I never should have agreed to this. But I did and now I can't get out of it, not without ruining everything for Gage."

"Speaking of parents," Ashley said.

Megan shook her head.

Her sister frowned. "You have to tell Mom."

Megan was horrified by the thought. "No, I don't."

"She'll never forgive you if she hears about it from someone else."

"She's in Switzerland with Edward until Ashley's wedding," Megan reminded her. "That's one of the reasons I finally agreed to go along with Gage's plan, because she won't be back until this charade is over."

"One of the reasons?" Paige queried.

Megan had told her cousin and her sister the truth about the engagement because they were her closest friends, but she hadn't told them about her plans to get naked and horizontal with her temporary fiancé.

After all, there were some things that even best friends didn't need to know.

Chapter Eleven

Megan had been wearing Gage's ring for three weeks and while they'd been spending a lot of time together both in and out of the lab, Gage hadn't once kissed her like he had the night they got engaged. He'd promised to teach her about male-female interactions, but she felt that her greatest lesson so far had been in sexual frustration.

"Want to grab some dinner?" Gage asked her as they were leaving the lab Friday night.

Meg shook her head. "I want to go home with you."

"For dinner?"

She couldn't blame him for being confused. After all, he hadn't been privy to the mental debate she'd waged with herself over the past several hours. Which meant that she would have to be a little more explicit about what she wanted.

"For sex," she said bluntly.

He stared at her.

"I just feel like I've been waiting and wondering for long enough. Now I just want to get it over with."

"Well, that's an enthusiastic endorsement."

She felt her cheeks flare. "I'm sorry. I am enthused. I really want to do this."

"But?"

How did he always seem to know when she was holding something back? And why couldn't he just take her up on her offer so that she could stop stressing over the details of what might or might not happen?

"But…I'm afraid I'll be disappointed."

His brows lifted.

"Not because of you," she said hastily. "I'm sure you're very good. Spectacular even."

"Thank you for that," he said drily.

Her cheeks burned hotter. "You're making fun of me."

"I'm not," he denied. "I'm just wondering why you're so anxious to get to something you expect will be disappointing."

"It's not that I expect it to be," she denied. "But…Bill said I had…unrealistic expectations."

"Unrealistic expectations?"

She nodded.

He seemed to consider that for a moment before asking, "Did you want to do it upside down on a trapeze?"

"No. Of course not." How could he even ask her that? Obviously she was way out of her league with Gage Richmond and crazy to even think about having sex with a man like him.

"Well, that's good," he said. "Because I don't have a trapeze."

"You're making fun of me again, aren't you?"

He smiled. "A little. But only because you're taking this so seriously."

"Not everyone thinks of sex as fun and games," she said, just a little primly.

"Maybe if more people did, there would be fewer disappointments." He took her hands, squeezed gently. "Do you trust me, Meg?"

She nodded without hesitation.

"Then trust that we'll get around to it, when the time is right."

She was disappointed by his response…and unexpectedly relieved. So she nodded again. "Okay."

He touched his lips to hers. "So how about pizza tonight?"

"Pizza sounds great."

It took more willpower than Gage would have thought he possessed to turn down Megan's offer. But while the words were what he wanted to hear, the way she blurted them out warned that she wasn't as certain about what she wanted as she tried to appear. And while he wanted her desperately, he didn't want her resigned, he wanted her aroused.

He didn't doubt that she was looking for sexual experience, but he also didn't doubt that she lacked such experience because she wasn't the type of woman to give herself to a man easily or lightly. Which meant that he was going to have to keep a tight rein on his own wants and needs until he was certain that she wanted him as much as he wanted her.

And maybe he was partly responsible for her apprehension. He'd been so careful not to push that he'd avoided touching her, worried that if he started, he wouldn't be able to stop. But he realized now that because he'd been keeping his distance from her, she was immediately nervous when he got too close.

The key, he knew, was to get her to relax so that she wasn't thinking about what might or might not happen, so that things evolved naturally.

So they did go for pizza—and they took it back to his place.

It was only the second time she'd been there, the first being the night that he'd put the engagement ring on her finger. Usually when they were together, it was at a restaurant or a movie theater or some other public place. Sometimes they would hang out at her house, usually with her sister and sometimes her cousin, but even if they were alone, the knowledge that Ashley might come in at any time was enough to hold his urges in check. He'd deliberately not taken her back to his place because he wasn't sure he could withstand the temptation of being alone with her.

But over the next couple of weeks, he took her to his home several more times to share a meal, maybe some wine and conversation. The first few times she was in his condo, she jolted every time he touched her, as if she expected he was going to jump her. But by the beginning of the second week, she had grown accustomed to the casual brush of his hand against her thigh, the lazy caress of a fingertip trailing down her arm.

But as she was becoming more comfortable with him, he was becoming distinctly more *un*comfortable. It seemed that he couldn't touch her without ending up with a raging hard-on. And when they sat on his sofa making out like teenagers, he worried that he was going to embarrass himself like a teenager in the backseat of his dad's car.

When Megan started initiating the touching and kissing, he figured that was a pretty clear sign that he'd been patient long enough.

He scooped her into his arms.

Megan's eyes went wide. "I thought this was something that only happened in movies and books."

He grinned. "In movies and books and in real-life moments when a man has been pushed to the limits of his endurance."

Her lips curved as she leaned her head back against his shoulder. "Are we going to have sex now?"

"I think that's a pretty good bet."

Her smile wavered, just a little. "I don't want you to feel like you have to do this," she said. "I mean, if it's not what you want."

"Why would you think it's not what I want?"

"Well, I've been thinking about our agreement, and I realized it really wasn't fair to use sex as a bargaining chip."

"I'm not complaining," he assured her.

"I just don't want you to worry that I'll renege on our deal if you want to change the terms."

"I don't want to change the terms. What I want is *you*." He kissed her softly, deeply. "I want you, Megan," he said again. "And it has nothing to do with the bargain we made and everything to do with the fact that you are a beautiful, smart, sexy woman—even if you are oblivious to the fact that you are a beautiful, smart, sexy woman."

She just blinked.

He tried not to smile, but there was something supremely satisfying about managing to shut down that fascinating brain of hers.

He took advantage of the moment and captured her mouth in another long, deep kiss.

"I'd like you to stay with me tonight." He whispered the words against her lips. "Tell me you want to stay."

Megan had never wanted anything more.

"I want to stay," she told Gage, and was rewarded with another kiss.

Her eyes drifted shut as he deepened the kiss. His lips trailed down her throat, his teeth scraping over tender skin. She shivered, surprised and aroused, and surprised that she was aroused.

She'd been so preoccupied by his mouth she hadn't realized he'd unfastened the buttons down the front of her blouse until he pushed the fabric over her shoulders, down her arms, trapping them in the sleeves, holding her immobile while that wickedly talented mouth kissed the slope of one breast, then the other, then nuzzled the hollow between them.

It was torture—incredibly delicious torture.

Clearly the man was a master at bedroom games, as the rumors alleged, because she didn't even know how the rest of her clothes ended up on the floor. But suddenly she was naked and he was easing her back down onto the bed, still kissing and touching her and generally making every hormone in her body sit up and beg.

Her breasts—small though they were—had received some attention before. Some clumsy gropes and sweaty-palmed pinches. Gage was neither clumsy nor sweaty. Nor did he seem disappointed by her size. His thumbs slowly circled around the outer edge of her nipples, moving slowly closer to the rigid peaks that were aching for his touch.

"Please." It was a sigh as much as a plea.

"Tell me what you want, Megan."

She shook her head, because she didn't know. She only knew that she wanted more, and yet, she didn't want to stop the exquisite pleasure of what he was doing right now.

But Gage didn't need her to give him step-by-step directions. It was readily apparent to her that he knew his way around her body better than she did. Of course, a man of his experience would, but she wasn't going to worry about that now. In fact, she wasn't going to worry about anything—

She sucked in a breath as his thumbs brushed over her nipples again.

"Do you like that?"

She could only nod.

Then he gently rolled her nipples between his fingers, and she gasped at the exquisite, piercing pleasure that shot through her system.

She hadn't realized that she'd closed her eyes until they flew open again at the shock of his mouth on her breast.

It was just the tip of his tongue, actually, but—oh, my—her eyes crossed as it swirled around the peak. Instinctively, she arched toward him, urging him to take more. And then his lips closed around the hard pebble of her nipple and he sucked hard.

She cried out in shocked pleasure, her hips rocking against him. She could feel the press of his erection against the jeans he still wore, and she wondered if he was as ready as she was, why he wasn't stripping the last of his clothes away to get on with it.

He groaned as he grabbed on to her hips, stilling their movements. "Are you trying to end this before we've begun?"

She felt her cheeks flush. "I thought…I mean…don't you want to…do it?"

His hands slid up her torso, skimming gently, reassuring. "I very definitely want to," he said, and touched his lips to hers in a brief but potent kiss. "But there are other things I want to do first." He paused, letting her consider that. "If you don't have any objection."

Other things? What kind of other things?

She wasn't sure she could take any more, but she would never know if she didn't take this chance.

"Oh, uh, no," she finally replied. "No objection."

"Good," he said, then shifted again to give the same exquisite attention to her other breast.

And while his mouth was busy at her breast, his hands were exploring elsewhere. Trailing down her ribs, over her hips, her legs, then moving upward again. He stroked the tender skin on the inside of her thighs now, his fingertips dancing softly over the skin in a teasing caress that had her muscles quivering.

Then he touched her, just the lightest brush of his fingertips against the moist nub at the apex of her legs, and she shattered. She simply flew apart like shards of a broken glass—an experience that was so sharp and intense it was almost painful.

When she finally stopped trembling, she noticed that he was holding her close.

"Oh, Meg." He nibbled gently on her earlobe. "You are…incredible."

She blinked, uncomprehending. "But I didn't do anything. It was you—"

He silenced her with a kiss, deep and hot and hungry, and she felt the sharp edge of desire rise up in her again.

"You said no objections, right?"

She nodded, though she didn't understand why he was asking now. Hadn't he already shown her everything—

She gasped again when his head disappeared between her legs.

Apparently he hadn't shown her everything.

His tongue stroked.

His lips nibbled.

She couldn't stand it…it was too much…so many layers of sensation…so much more than she'd ever dreamed.

Even as her body shuddered with the aftershocks of another orgasm, she felt as if something was missing, somehow she still wanted.

He let go of her only long enough to finally strip away his clothes and take care of protection. And then he lifted her hips and eased into her. Slowly. Gently. And, oh, so perfectly.

"Are you okay?"

She was surprised—and touched—that after everything he'd already done to ensure her pleasure, he would even think to ask. She could see the strain on his face, felt it in the arms that held him rigid over top of her as he waited for her response.

She slid her hands up his arms, felt his muscles quiver. "I'm okay," she assured him, and drew his head down to hers.

Gage sank into the kiss, and into her.

She might not have been a virgin, but Megan was undoubtedly the most innocent woman he'd ever taken to his bed.

Innocent yet eager, and that was an unexpectedly arousing combination, and one that had nerves and guilt gnawing at him. But the nerves and guilt were no match for a desire that had been building for too long, and his body was already straining with the effort of holding itself in check.

This was all she wanted from him, and he was determined to make the experience a memorable one for her. But then she wrapped her legs around him, pulling him deeper inside her. She smiled in response to his groan, a little shyly, as if she was only beginning to realize the effect she had on him. Heaven help him if she ever truly discovered her power.

Then she started to move, instinctively thrusting her hips in a rhythm as old as time itself, and though he desperately tried to grasp for the last slippery threads of control, they slipped right through his fingers. When she rose up again, he plunged into her. Deeper, harder, faster. He was like a wild animal finally set free from its cage, desperately, mindlessly racing to the finish.

If he'd been able to think, he might have worried that she was shocked, even appalled, by his behavior. But she met him thrust for thrust and spurred him on with her deep moans and throaty murmurs. Then she cried out and the tight clench of her muscles drained everything he had left, and he emptied himself into her.

Megan had known that having sex with Gage would be an experience.

That was, after all, one of her primary reasons for going along with his engagement plan. She wasn't looking for love—she just wanted to know what all the hype was about, because in her limited experience sex had never been more than a brief and somewhat pleasant interlude. She'd experienced desire and anticipation, and disappointment, though she'd never been certain if the lack had been in herself or her partner, or if—as Bill Penske had claimed—her expectations were simply too high.

Gage Richmond changed all of her perceptions.

He'd shown her that sex was about the journey as much as the destination, and he'd shown her how to enjoy every step along the way.

Her lips curved as she thought about how very much she had enjoyed every step along the way. "Thank you."

He propped himself up on an elbow. "What exactly are you thanking me for?"

"For keeping your end of the bargain."

"I'm nothing if not a man of my word," he assured her solemnly.

"And I appreciate the experience. I think I have a slightly better understanding of everything now."

"You think so?"

She nodded.

"Maybe we should go over things again." He stroked a hand down her torso, his fingertips dancing lightly, teasingly, over her skin. "Just to be sure."

She shivered, goose bumps rising on her flesh even as her blood heated in her veins. She wouldn't have thought it was possible for desire to stir again, but apparently she still had some things to learn. "Well, if you think that's necessary."

He opened another condom, rolled it into place. "I think—" his lips brushed against hers, once, twice, as he levered his body over hers again, eased into her "—it's very definitely necessary."

Chapter Twelve

It was unusual for Gage to wake up and not be alone in his bed. Though he had a reputation—not entirely undeserved—for having been with a lot of women, he wasn't in the habit of actually spending the night with them. The darkest hours were usually his alone, and that he'd let Megan stay—had, in fact, not even considered taking her home—implied a greater degree of intimacy than he was accustomed to, that he wasn't sure he was ready for.

So when he woke up Saturday morning and discovered that her back was snuggled against his front, he experienced the slightest hint of panic. When he realized *his* arm was around *her,* the panic escalated.

He needed coffee to clear his head and space so that he could think, and he wouldn't get either if he gave in to the urge to slip his hand up to cover her small, firm breast or nuzzle the tender skin on her throat that he'd learned was ultra-sensitive to the rasp of his shadowed cheek.

With more haste than care, he extricated himself from the covers and slipped out of the bed.

On a diagram of the human body, Megan could accurately identify every muscle. She just wasn't certain she had ever actually used them all before.

When she woke up the morning after the night she'd spent in Gage's bed, she knew she had, because every single muscle ached. But it wasn't at all an unpleasant feeling, more of a revelation. She'd never realized the human body was capable of giving so much…taking so much…feeling so much.

She knew the night had meant a lot more to her than it had to Gage, and she accepted that. When this engagement was over, it was unlikely he would even think about her, never mind the night they'd spent together.

But she would remember it forever.

Because Gage had shown her so much more than the mechanics of pleasurable sex—although he'd done that, too, and in spectacular fashion. He'd shown her what it meant to really be connected to someone else. And for that period of time where their bodies were linked together, when she could feel the beat of his heart in sync with her own, she felt as if they fit.

Of course it was an illusion, she knew that. The connection was purely physical and probably only in her own mind, but still, the one night they'd spent together had exceeded all of her expectations, and she would always be grateful to him for that.

Just as Gage didn't usually sleep with his lovers, he didn't cook cozy breakfasts for them, either. And yet Megan was there, seated across from him at the table, eating bacon he'd fried and eggs he'd scrambled, drinking coffee he'd brewed. And looking as if she belonged.

He shook his head, as if doing so could rid it of that incongruous thought.

She was the type of woman who was all about strings and he had no intention of getting tangled up. Of course, the ring on her finger suggested otherwise, but they both knew the truth. It was, as she'd described, a prop, nothing more. And they didn't have a relationship, they had an agreement. An agreement with a specific and clearly defined purpose.

He nibbled on a piece of bacon and decided that he was overreacting. After all, one breakfast didn't make a relationship. Even one breakfast after a night of spectacular sex didn't make a relationship. So he would simply enjoy her company along with his eggs and, when the meal was done, he'd take her home, clearly reestablishing the boundaries.

It was a good plan. Except that after breakfast, she insisted on helping with the cleanup and he found the image of her up to her wrists in soapy water strangely arousing, and the next thing he knew they were back upstairs and naked in his bed.

Megan was late for Sunday brunch.

In fact, she almost forgot about it entirely until Gage suggested that they should go somewhere to eat because he was out of bread and milk. He didn't seem to mind that she'd asked for a ride to the café, though he did grumble about not being invited to eat with them. But Sunday brunch was a sacred and exclusive ritual for the three women, and Megan had no intention of letting that change, even if she had been tempted to skip the event altogether.

But the truth was, the whole weekend with Gage had been incredible, and incredibly intense, and she was grateful for the excuse to take a step back, to give herself space to breathe. Because she was very much afraid that if she didn't take that step now, it might be too late.

"Well, look who finally decided to show up," Ashley said when Megan slid into the empty chair beside her.

Megan felt her cheeks burning. "Sorry." Then, to the waiter who immediately came over to fill her cup with coffee, she said, "Thank you."

Paige waved a hand dismissively. "Please don't apologize. If I'd spent the morning having hot, sweaty sex with a man like Gage Richmond, I definitely wouldn't be here now."

"How do you know I spent the morning having hot, sweaty sex?"

"The tousled hair and fresh beard burn on your neck are dead giveaways," Paige informed her. "Not to mention the thoroughly satisfied gleam in your eyes."

"Jeez, is it really that obvious?"

"Only to those of us who aren't getting any."

While Ashley smiled at Paige's comment, she couldn't quite hide the worry in her eyes. "I'm glad things are going well," she said to her sister. "Just…be careful."

"Always," Megan promised her.

Ashley shook her head. "I'm not talking about birth control."

"If you're worried that I'm going to fall in love, don't be," Megan said. "We have an agreement."

"Love isn't something that can be scheduled or

planned or contracted out of," Paige interjected. "Believe me, I've written a lot of prenups and settlement agreements and the human heart isn't bound by any precedents or statutes."

"Okay then, let's just say that I have no illusions about our relationship, and no expectations beyond the terms of our agreement."

"But he is going to the reunion with you?"

Megan nodded. "He didn't even hesitate when I asked. Apparently the ring on my finger is an implied escort for any occasion."

Her cousin sighed. "I think I'm going to skip it."

"If I have to go, you have to go," Megan said.

"We're all going," Ashley said firmly.

"But I haven't found anyone to go with me and I refuse to be the only one of us without a date."

"I'll be your date," Ashley said.

"Won't Trevor have something to say about that?"

"If he does, we won't hear it all the way from South Carolina."

Megan frowned at that. "Trevor's not going to the reunion?"

Ashley shook her head.

"Why not?"

"A bunch of guys from his office are going to Myrtle Beach for a charity golf tournament that weekend."

"And he couldn't miss it?" Paige asked incredulously.

"He didn't want to miss it."

"But he'll miss your reunion."

"It's *my* reunion," Ashley said, a little defensively.

"And he's *your* fiancé," Paige pointed out.

When Ashley looked away, Megan knew her sister was more bothered by her fiancé's defection than she wanted to let on.

In light of Ashley's recent comments about Trevor withdrawing, she worried that his choice of golf over the reunion was just further proof of the fact. And she couldn't help but feel a little bit guilty that she was so happy while her sister obviously was not.

The main foyer of the school was set up as the primary check-in point, and from there they were directed to specific classrooms, depending on graduation year.

"I thought you were a couple years younger than your sister," Gage said to Megan as they followed Ashley and Paige to Room 131.

"Three years," she told him.

"But you graduated the same year?"

"I was accelerated through school," she admitted.

"Then you're probably even younger than I guessed."

"What was your guess?"

"Oh, no. I'm not getting caught in that trap."

She laughed. "Okay, I'll tell you. I'm twenty-five."

"When is your birthday?"

"February second."

"I should have known that. As your fiancé, I mean."

"We weren't engaged in February."

"My birthday's in October," he told her.

"And our engagement will almost be over by then," she said, reminding herself of the fact as they entered what had once been her tenth-grade math class.

But when Megan spotted Tara Gallagher standing inside the door and saw the way the other woman's eyes widened when she walked in with Gage, she couldn't deny the pride and possessiveness that surged inside of her. Maybe he was only hers for a while, but she was definitely going to enjoy every second of it.

After receiving their name tags, Megan and Gage headed to the gymnasium where the band was playing songs intended to evoke memories of high school events. But of course, Megan had never attended any. In fact, she'd only ever planned to go to one dance, and only then because she'd been invited.

Darrin Walsh had been the captain of the football team and her chemistry lab partner and she'd been so speechless when he'd asked if she wanted to go to the Spring Fling with him, she'd only been able to nod.

The night of the dance, she'd waited at the door so long the excited butterflies in her stomach had slowly died with last pitiful little flutters. It was barely ten o'clock, two hours before their midnight curfew, that Ashley and Paige came home. Having seen Darrin stroll into the gym with Tara, they'd immediately guessed what had happened.

But Megan had still refused to believe it, and she'd spent the weekend by the phone, waiting for him to call and explain. It was only when the phone remained silent, and when she heard the whispers and snickers as she made her way through the halls Monday morning, that she finally accepted the truth.

The memory wasn't a good one, but as Megan walked into the gym with Gage, it wasn't as powerful or upsetting as it once had been. And it dimmed even further as Gage stayed close to her side through the evening.

But after a couple of drinks and a few dances, she had to excuse herself to use the ladies' room. When she came back out again and recognized Darrin Walsh across the room, her heart didn't skip a beat and her knees didn't tremble, and she finally accepted that she wasn't the same shy, scared girl she'd been ten years earlier.

Still, she was surprised when he crossed the room to

approach her. She didn't think he would have recognized her and, even if he had, he certainly wouldn't have gone out of his way to speak with her.

Her suspicion was confirmed when his gaze dropped to the name tag pinned to her dress, then his eyes went wide.

"Megan Roarke." His eyes swept over her, boldly, appreciatively. "Wow. You grew up."

"It happens to most of us," she told him.

"But…wow," he said again.

A few months earlier, she wouldn't have been able to endure such blatant perusal without turning away, she wouldn't have known how to respond to such a compliment without stuttering. But being with Gage had gone a long way to building her self-confidence.

"And you're as eloquent as always," she told him.

He smiled, appreciative of the compliment, oblivious to her sarcasm. "You went away to school, didn't you?"

She nodded. "Northwestern."

"What are you doing now?"

"I'm a senior lab tech at Richmond Pharmaceuticals."

"Wow," he said for a third time. "I can't believe it's really you."

And she couldn't believe she'd ever seen anything in a guy who couldn't stop staring at her breasts long enough to focus on a conversation. Of course, that hadn't been a problem in high school because she hadn't had any breasts back then.

"What are you up to these days?" she asked, because it seemed impolite not to.

He rolled back his shoulders, puffed out his chest. "I'm coaching football."

"Congratulations," she said, unable to think of any other response.

"The boys had a tough year last season, but we're building a strong team for next fall."

She nodded. Although she'd once gone starry eyed over a certain football player, she'd never understood or cared about the game.

Darrin nodded, too. He started to lift his beer bottle to his mouth, then paused. "Hey, can I buy you a drink? I mean, it's probably the least I can do in exchange for all the help you gave me in high school."

"No, thanks," she said, zeroing in on Gage as he made his way toward her.

The way her heart bumped in response to the smile on his face told her she was treading on dangerous ground with her fake fiancé, but she was too relieved and grateful to worry about that now.

"Are you here by yourself?" Darrin asked.

The question drew her attention back to the man she'd forgotten was at her side just as Gage joined them.

Whether he'd accurately summed up the scene or was just intent on playing his part, her fiancé dipped his head to kiss her full on the lips.

"Oh, uh, obviously not," Darrin answered his own question.

"This is—" the words *my fiancé* stuck in her throat, so Megan amended her planned introduction "—Gage Richmond." Then to Gage, she said, "Darrin and I were in twelfth-grade chemistry together."

"I was just thanking Roarke for her help in that chemistry class. I wouldn't have got through it without her." Then, waving to someone else across the room, he said. "Well, I'm going to go catch up with Toby Bell."

Megan watched him go and felt as if she might finally have put the past behind her.

"Did I interrupt?" Gage asked, sounding more amused than concerned.

She shook her head. "In fact, your timing was perfect."

"Were you really his study partner in high school?"

"Not exactly."

He lifted a brow.

"I wrote up all of his lab reports and let him copy off of my tests." She shrugged. "He was the quarterback of the football team and I was foolishly and hopelessly in love.

"Of course, he didn't even recognize me," she confessed. "He only knew my name because he read it on my name tag."

Gage scowled. "No doubt he came out of his way to…read your name tag."

"It seems strange being here," she admitted. "I feel like a fraud."

"Why?"

"Because this isn't me. It doesn't matter what I'm wearing on the outside—inside I'm still the same 'Roarke the Dork' I was in high school."

Gage tipped her chin up, forcing her to meet his gaze. "You've only got it half right," he said. "The reason it doesn't matter what you're wearing is because you've always been an incredibly beautiful woman hiding behind your brain."

"The way you say it almost makes me believe it's true."

"Let me convince you," he said, and bent his head to kiss her.

His lips were soft but firm as they moved over hers in a slow, sensuous exploration that made her heart pound and her body yearn. His tongue slid into her mouth, not deeply probing but gently teasing, and her blood heated in her veins, melting any last token resistance. Her hands moved up his chest, over his shoulders. He splayed his hand against the small of her back, drawing her closer, close enough so that she could tell he was as aroused as she was.

When he finally eased his mouth from hers, she was breathless and just a little dazed. "What was that for?"

"Partly to convince you. Partly because I really wanted a taste of you." He grinned. "But mostly because I want all of the guys here to know who you're going home with tonight."

Maybe she should have been offended by the arrogant and very public way he'd staked his claim, but she was too aroused to be angry.

"Speaking of going home," she said.

His smile widened. "You read my mind. But we should have one last dance before we go." He led her to the floor where several couples were already swaying to the tune of an old Madonna ballad.

Megan melted into his arms, thinking she was seriously crazy for him, and that had never been part of the plan.

Ashley wished she'd never badgered Megan into accepting the invitation to their high school reunion, because then she wouldn't have felt compelled to come. But she'd wanted to attend the reunion, and she'd assumed that Trevor would be with her. She couldn't have guessed that her fiancé would choose a weekend golf trip with the guys over her.

So she'd come with Paige. But shortly after their arrival, her cousin had struck up a conversation with Marvin Tedeschi—former yearbook editor and chess club champion—and they'd been inseparable ever since.

Sure there were other people for Ashley to talk to and

hang out with. She'd been one of the popular girls in high school, part of the in-crowd and friends with almost everyone one, so it seemed that she couldn't turn around without seeing someone else who wanted to reminisce about the good old days with her.

Except that Ashley didn't feel much like reminiscing. She'd thought that coming to the reunion would be her chance to face her broken dreams and ancient heartache and finally put them behind her. She'd also thought that she'd be facing those broken dreams and ancient heartache with Trevor by her side, and his absence just made her all the more aware of everything that was missing.

At least there was a bar, she thought philosophically, as she made her way toward it. She ordered a glass of chardonnay, figuring she would sip at it for an hour or so while she mingled, then quietly slip away.

She spotted Megan and Gage dancing and smiled. Regardless of their reasons for being together, there was no denying how well they fit, even if neither of them was ready to admit it.

As she turned away from the couples on the dance floor, she found herself face-to-face with Cameron Turcotte.

"Hello, Ashley."

She tightened her grip on her wineglass and forced a smile, because she absolutely refused to let him see how much his unexpected presence had rattled her. "Cameron. I didn't expect to see you here."

"This was my high school, too," he reminded her.

As if she needed reminding. As if just seeing him again didn't open the floodgates on too many memories she'd tried for so long to forget.

"You came all the way from Seattle for a high school

reunion?" she asked, hoping to sound both disbelieving and disinterested.

"Actually, I happened to be in town for a meeting," he admitted. "It was just lucky that the timing worked out."

Lucky for him, maybe, and very unlucky for her. She lifted her glass to sip her wine, and refused to ask the question that was on her lips.

"My meeting was with Elijah Alexander," he told her, despite the fact that she hadn't asked.

The name was enough to confirm the rumor Paige had warned her about, that Dr. Alexander was looking toward retirement and was actively seeking someone to help out his local practice.

And though she wanted to continue to ignore him and the information he'd revealed, she heard herself say, "You're going to work with Dr. Alex?"

"I'm considering it," he agreed. "I wasn't sure how I would feel, coming back after so many years. Then I walked in here tonight and it was almost like the past twelve years had never happened."

Ashley only wished she could wipe those years from her mind so easily. But as hard as she'd tried, she couldn't forget, and she wasn't going to stroll down memory lane with the only man who had ever broken her heart. Instead she asked, "Did your wife make the trip with you?"

She'd learned, through a chance meeting with his mother at the grocery store, that he had married. At the time, the news had stunned her so much that she couldn't even remember if she'd responded to Gayle Turcotte's announcement. But that was a long time ago, and she spoke casually now, as if his marital status was of no concern to her. Because it wasn't.

"No." He looked away. "I'm divorced now."

"I'm sorry to hear it," she said.

He shrugged. "Things don't always turn out the way we plan."

"I know," she said pointedly. "I learned that lesson the hard way."

She started to move away, but he reached out and put his hand on her arm. It was a casual touch, but it froze her in place.

"I'm sorry, Ashley."

She shook his hand off, angry with him for stirring her up and angrier with herself for letting him. "What, exactly, are you sorry for?"

"Hurting you."

"It was a long time ago," she said dismissively.

"I'd like to explain."

"There's no need. Really."

"But…"

His words trailed off and she saw that his eyes were fixed on the ring nestled on the third finger of her left hand. Not nearly as eye-popping as her sister's, but just as significant.

"You're engaged."

He sounded both surprised and disappointed, a reaction that might have given her some sense of satisfaction if she wasn't feeling so much confusion about the meaning of the ring on her finger. "We're getting married in the fall," she told him.

"Well, then, I guess congratulations are in order."

"Thank you."

"Where is your fiancé?"

He looked around, as if expecting the man who'd put the ring on her finger would be somewhere nearby.

As he should have been, but Ashley forced that thought from her mind.

"Trevor had to be out of town this weekend."

"I'm sorry I won't get a chance to meet him—" his eyes met hers, held "—to tell him what a lucky guy he is."

"I'm sure he knows," she said, even though she wasn't sure of anything anymore.

Gage was leading Megan away from the crowd, anxious to get her alone—somewhere much more private—when she suddenly stopped moving.

"Oh, no." The words were barely more than a whisper but heartfelt.

He turned. "What's wrong?"

"Ashley."

His gaze moved in the direction Megan was looking, and he spotted her sister on the edge of the dance floor, talking to someone. "I don't see a problem."

"That's Cameron Turcotte."

"I still don't see the problem."

"There's some serious history there," Megan told him. "Cameron grew up across the street from us and Ashley dated him all through high school."

"What happened?"

"He dumped Ash when he went away to college."

"That's not an uncommon story," he said gently.

"I know," she admitted. "But Ashley really loved him. And he broke her heart. Completely."

"And it was a lot of years ago."

"I know," she said again. "And she's engaged to Trevor, and he's married to someone else, so maybe they're just reminiscing about old times but—"

Her words trailed off when Ashley turned away from Cameron.

Even Gage could see the tears that glittered in her sister's eyes, so he dropped the arm he'd settled around her shoulders and said, "Go."

She looked up at him, gratitude and regret reflected in the luminous depths of her violet eyes. "This isn't how I wanted the night to end," she told him.

It wasn't how he wanted it to end, either, but because he understood and appreciated her loyalty to her sister, he only kissed her gently. "Rain check?"

Her smile was soft and filled with promise. "You bet."

Chapter Thirteen

The following Friday, Gage and Megan played hooky from work—with the boss's approval, of course—and drove up to Lake Placid. Allan and Grace had a house on the water and had offered it to their youngest son for the weekend.

"To take a much-deserved break from the lab," Allan told Gage.

Which translated, Gage told Megan, into "a reward for finally acting like the son we want you to be."

Megan suspected Gage was too cynical, but regardless of the reason for the loan of the house, she couldn't get too excited about it. Because a romantic getaway wasn't quite so romantic when it was yet another act in a carefully staged play. And because she was all too aware that Gage had been carefully and deliberately withdrawing from her over the past week. Since the reunion, in fact.

She should have known it would happen. Their "engagement" had already, by his own admission, lasted longer than any other relationship he'd had in the past several years. Obviously he was starting to feel hemmed in. Or maybe he was just bored with her.

The latter possibility, though more depressing, was also more likely. Gage had dated a lot of beautiful, sophisticated and experienced women. She'd had a total of two lovers in her twenty-five years and while the passion she had shared with Gage seemed real and compelling to her, she didn't really have much basis for comparison.

But she did know that nothing else about their relationship was real. It was all about creating and maintaining an illusion, and this getaway was only the latest chapter in a book filled with lies and deceptions.

Still, she was determined to make the most of the weekend at the beautiful two-story, timber-frame house with huge arching windows that looked out over the water.

"The bedrooms are on the upper level," he said, as she followed him through the door.

Megan set her duffel bag at the foot of the stairs and traced his path into the kitchen.

While he put away the groceries they'd brought, she took a look around, admiring the glossy cherrywood cabinets, wide granite countertops and gleaming stainless-steel appliances. Beyond the breakfast nook was a pair of French doors that opened onto a covered deck.

"This place is amazing."

"I used to love coming here when Craig and I were kids," he told her. "But the older we got, the busier we got, and our trips were fewer and farther between. To tell the truth, I can't even remember the last time I was here."

"Or who you were with?" she wondered aloud.

"No, that I'm certain of. It was either my parents or just me and Craig. I've never been here with anyone else." He closed the fridge and smiled at her. "I told you my parents like you."

Which, instead of reassuring Megan, only made her feel worse about her part in his deception.

"What do you want to do?" he asked. "We could go into the village or walk down to the lake or just flake out in front of the television."

"Don't worry about me," she said. "You don't have to entertain me every minute of every day."

He frowned. "We came here to spend the weekend together."

"Only because your parents suggested it."

"And because you're my fiancée," he reminded her.

"I wasn't sure you remembered that part."

His frown deepened. "What is that supposed to mean?"

"Give me a little credit, Gage. I may be naive and inexperienced, but even I can tell that you've lost interest in me."

"Where in hell did you ever get an idea like that?" he demanded.

She met his gaze evenly. "From you."

"What did I do?"

"It's not what you did but what you didn't do."

"Okay—what didn't I do?"

She didn't think she would have to spell it out for him, and though she felt her cheeks flame, she wasn't going to back down. "You haven't touched me in more than a week."

He stared at her, as if he didn't quite understand what she was saying. "That's why you're pissed off at me? Because we haven't had sex in a week?"

"It's been more than a week," she said again. "And

I'm not peeved. Okay, I am peeved. But only because I thought, our arrangement notwithstanding, that you respected me enough to be honest with me."

"Honey, right now I am honestly confused."

She huffed out a breath. "You should have told me you didn't want me anymore."

"I haven't stopped wanting you," he insisted. "And maybe that's the problem."

It was a statement that left her as confused as he claimed to be.

"When we first agreed on the terms of this arrangement, I was certain that the attraction I felt for you would run its course," he told her. "Because that's what always happened before.

"But the more I had you, the more I wanted you. And the more I asked of you, the more you gave. And the more you gave, the guiltier I felt because I knew I was taking advantage of our agreement and your innocence."

His explanation annoyed rather than appeased her. "Then maybe I should be feeling guilty for taking advantage of our agreement and your experience."

He shook his head, dismissing her twisted logic. "The guilt should have been my first clue."

"Clue to what?"

"That I have feelings for you."

Megan's heart gave an unexpected bump against her ribs. Her annoyance faded.

I have feelings for you.

It was hardly a declaration of undying love and yet she knew the words were sincere because of his reluctance to say them. And a tentative hope began to blossom deep in her heart.

"Okay, so maybe we could both scrap the guilt and figure out where we go from here," she suggested lightly.

"I don't want anything more than I wanted when I put that ring on your finger," Gage told her.

She understood that it was more a warning than a statement, and she nodded. "Nothing has to change."

Except they both knew everything already had.

And when Gage pulled Megan into his arms, he knew that she knew it. But it was easier for him—maybe for both of them—to pretend otherwise.

They'd been lovers for weeks now, but in some ways, she was still so innocent, so unaware of her own appeal. And although he'd been certain his desire for her would be sated once he'd finally had her, the truth was, he wanted her more.

And never so desperately as at that very moment.

They left a trail of discarded clothes on the way up to the bedroom, then tumbled together onto the bed, mouths fused, limbs tangled.

He wanted to take his time, to savor her. But the desire stirring inside of him was too strong, too fierce. It had been—as she'd deliberately pointed out—more than a week since they'd been together, but he felt as if he'd been waiting for her forever.

Usually, after about three weeks with a woman, he started to feel claustrophobic. He didn't feel like that with Megan. Maybe it was because they'd already agreed to an end date for their relationship, at the end of which they would go their separate ways. That six-month deadline meant he could enjoy the time they had together without worrying that she would expect more.

Or maybe it was just Megan.

He had no idea where that thought had come from, and he sure as hell didn't want to think about what it meant, so he shoved it aside as he skimmed his hands over her. He felt her arch, heard her moan, and knew she was as desperate for him as he was for her. He drove into her, and swallowed her cries of pleasure as they rode out the storm of desire that had overtaken them both.

Afterward, as he drifted toward sleep with Megan tucked close to his side, he acknowledged that his feelings for her were stronger and deeper than anything he'd ever felt for another woman. But still, he could choose what to do with those feelings—or he could choose to do nothing at all. Because his heart was and would always be his own.

This time when he woke in the morning, Gage expected to find Megan in bed beside him and was disappointed when she wasn't. And then he was annoyed to realize he was disappointed.

Dammit, what was it about this one woman that seemed to tie him up in knots?

Having worked with Megan the past couple of years, albeit indirectly, he'd thought he had a pretty good understanding of her character.

She was smart. Smarter than anyone he'd ever known, that had been obvious straight away. But the more he got to know her, the more he understood that her intelligence was only one layer of the whole—and not even the most important one. She was loyal to her friends and family. She was compassionate and caring, generous with both her time and her affection, and she was the most incredibly responsive lover he'd ever had.

And he was in way over his head.

She'd asked him to be honest with her last night, and he'd been more honest than he'd intended. But there was one truth he'd held back—that the depth of his feelings for her absolutely terrified him.

Rather than examine those feelings too closely, he heeded the rumbling of his stomach and headed to the kitchen in search of some breakfast.

What he found was Megan, standing in front of the stove and wrapped in a short, silky robe that outlined every delicious curve of her body.

"I thought you didn't cook."

She jolted at the sound of his voice from the doorway, but when she turned, she was smiling.

"I don't," she insisted. "At least not very well. And not very often, if I can help it. But I was hungry and the box said 'just add water,' so I thought it was maybe something I could tackle."

He watched her slide the spatula into the frying pan, lift the pancake and flip it.

"Are you tackling enough to share?" he asked.

"I think so," she said, and gestured to the oven.

He peeked through the glass window and saw that there was a plate already piled high with pancakes that were being kept warm.

"How much mix did you use?"

"About half the box."

He chuckled. "Looks like you've made breakfast and lunch and maybe dinner."

"Breakfast and lunch," she allowed. "But I think we'll need something with a little more substance for dinner."

"We could always fry up some bacon to go with the pancakes."

Without so much as a glance in his direction, she flipped the next pancake at his head.

Of course, he had to exact revenge for that insult with a passionate kiss that went on so long that they forgot who was the punisher and who was being punished. Then they finally ate some of the pancakes—barely making a dent in the stack Megan had cooked—and tidied up the kitchen together.

"Do you want to take a walk into the village today?" he asked when the last of the dishes had been dried and put away.

She looked out the window. "It's raining."

"So? It will be an easy way for you to get that wet look you like."

Her smile was wry. "I can't believe you remembered that."

"It was a memorable moment."

"Then you should also remember that my teeth were chattering when I said it."

"It's a light spring drizzle today," he said. "But if you're afraid of a little rain, we could drive, instead."

Her eyes narrowed, as he knew they would. He'd never known Megan to back down from a challenge.

"I think I'd like to walk."

He grinned and took her hand.

They were both wet and chilled when they got back from their trip to the village, so Gage started a fire while Megan went upstairs to change into dry clothes. By the time she came back down in a pair of softly faded jeans and a bulky wool sweater, the flames were crackling.

She sat beside him on the floor in front of the fireplace and he handed her one of the glasses of wine he'd poured.

"This is nice," she said.

"Romantic?"

She smiled. "Definitely."

"A guy doesn't go to this much effort for a woman unless he's still interested," he told her.

"Or at least interested in getting in her pants, my mother would say."

"That, too," he agreed. Then, because she'd given him the opening and he was curious, he asked, "What is the story with you and your mom, anyway?"

Megan leaned her head back against his shoulder, still facing the fire. "There's not really a story," she said. "We just don't understand one another. I think she was completely baffled by me from the moment I was born and we've never quite managed to get past that."

"What about your dad? You never talk about him."

"He died a few weeks before my high school graduation."

"Were you close to him?"

She was silent for a moment, and when she finally spoke, her voice was thick with emotion. "He was everything to me. Parent, friend, confidant. And he loved me unconditionally."

He hugged her closer.

"He died in a car accident," she told him. "I remember the last time I saw him—I was sitting at the kitchen table, eating breakfast when he dropped a kiss on the top of my head and said he'd see me at dinner. But he didn't. He never came home."

"I'm sorry," he said gently.

She nodded. "He was a good man. A good father. And as much as I don't see eye-to-eye with my mother, I know she loved him, even if it took me a long time to realize how much.

"After he died, I went away to school so I didn't really see how devastated she was. And when she started dating again, a few years later, I was angry with her because I thought she was trying to replace him.

"It seemed like every time I came home, she was

dating someone new. But she never dated anyone for too long, she never let anyone get too close. It took me a long time to realize she wasn't fickle, she was ensuring she didn't fall in love. Because so long as she didn't fall in love again, she couldn't have her heart broken again.

"Of course, now she's in Switzerland with her latest boyfriend, so my theory could be wrong."

"Or maybe she's just finally ready to move on," he suggested.

She turned around so that she was facing him, and he took a moment to study her in the light of the fire. Her hair was still damp from the rain, her face was completely bare of makeup, and the oversize sweater disguised her feminine curves, and yet to Gage, she was the most naturally beautiful woman he'd ever known.

Her eyes, those gorgeous violet eyes that he knew would haunt him until the end of his days, were serious and intense. "Can I ask you a question now?"

"Sure."

"When are *you* going to be ready to move on?"

Megan wasn't surprised that Gage didn't answer, that he only looked past her, to the flames flickering and crackling in the grate.

"I didn't even realize it until I was talking out loud," she told him. "But your dating pattern is just like my mother's. You never date anyone for more than a few months, and you never let anyone get too close."

"Says the woman wearing the ring I put on her finger," he noted, still not looking at her.

"Which you put there under false pretenses."

Now, finally, he shifted his gaze back to her, and the stark pain she saw in his eyes nearly took her breath away. "Don't."

She only wanted to understand, but the single word was an entreaty as much as a demand, and it was the plea she couldn't ignore.

"Okay," she said, accepting that the time for talking was over.

Then she lifted her arms to link them around his neck, pulling him down on the rug with her. That he didn't resist. And though it made her heart ache to realize that he wouldn't open up to her, that this was all he would accept from her, for now, it would be enough.

The following Friday night, Gage decided to toss some steaks on the grill and enjoy a quiet night at home with his temporary fiancée. A plan that he knew was unlikely to be realized as soon as Megan walked in the door, then slammed it shut behind her.

He started to offer her a glass of wine, but the look in her eye warned him that it was more likely he would wear it than she would drink it. He set the glass back down again.

"Hi, honey. How was your day?"

"How was my day?" Her eyes were narrowed and her tone was icy. "How can you ask me that you… manipulative…cretin."

They were probably the harshest words Gage had ever heard come out of her mouth, so he decided that it wouldn't be wise to let her see his amusement. Obviously she was worked up about something and though he didn't have a clue about what that might be, he held up both hands in mock surrender. "What did I do?"

"You lied to me about this engagement."

She paced across the living room, her low-heeled shoes clicking on the hardwood floor. But it was the hurt that she didn't quite manage to hide that echoed in his mind.

"It was never just about you needing to prove something to your father," she said now. "It was about wanting the V.P. office when Dean Garrison retires."

"I never made any secret about the fact that I expected to move up in the company," he reminded her, refusing to feel guilty about that fact.

"No, you didn't," she agreed. "You just failed to tell me that you wanted the same job I've been working toward for the past eighteen months."

He frowned. "I thought you were happy working on the research angle."

"Of course I'm happy. I love my job." Except the way she threw the words at him suggested otherwise. "But it's not what I want to do for the rest of my life."

"It's not?"

"That surprises you, doesn't it? That I might actually have ambitions."

"I never really thought about it," he admitted.

"And why would you?" she challenged. "Mousy little Megan should be happy to hide in the lab, avoiding all unnecessary contact with the big bad world."

"I certainly never thought *that.*"

"Well, you should have. Because it's true—or it was until I started working with you on this trial. You encouraged me to take the lead on the project, and you made me see that I could do it. To see that I was capable of doing so much more. And to realize that I *want* to do more. I don't just want to participate in the research, I want to determine the direction of it. I want to make a difference. And I could do that from the V.P. office. But you didn't even tell me that Dean Garrison was planning to retire."

He was silent for a moment, trying to sort through all of the information in her outburst, but in the end he only asked, "How did you find out?"

"*He* told me. I had my performance review today and Dean *raved* about my work. He told me I was an asset to the company. And he told me that he was going to recommend that I be considered for promotion when he retires at the end of the summer."

He should have been annoyed to hear that Garrison would make such a recommendation, but how could he be when he knew it was the right thing to do? Because Megan was undoubtedly an asset in the lab and to the company. And he felt a twinge of guilt that he'd completely ignored her ambitions to further his own.

"I was so excited when I walked out of his office," she continued, "and then I realized that his enthusiastic endorsement was nothing more than a pitiful consolation prize because the V.P. office is what you've been after all along. And there is no way the Board of Directors will promote an unknown lab researcher over someone named Richmond."

She glared at him through eyes that glittered with unshed tears. "Especially now that you've proven your maturity and responsibility by finding yourself an appropriate fiancée."

"You're right," Gage said, because there was really nothing else he could say. "I used you for my own purposes, without even considering what you wanted, and you have every right to be pissed."

"I just wanted a real shot at it." Megan spoke softly now, all of her anger drained away by his admission, her shoulders slumped with resignation. "I wanted my work to mean something."

It was the same thing he'd wanted—and the reason she was wearing his ring. He'd needed to neutralize his bad-boy reputation, to take it out of the equation so that the board of directors would look at his work

record instead of his personal life and put him in the
V.P. office.

She made her way back to the door, and his heart
started to pound harder, faster, an immediate and instinctive protest against the possibility that she might
actually walk out of his condo, walk out on *him*.

Don't go.

The words he wanted to speak lodged in his throat.

He wasn't a child anymore, heartbroken as he
watched his mother walk out the door. He wouldn't
plead, he wouldn't beg. Not this time.

If Megan didn't want to stay, he wasn't going to try
to convince her otherwise.

But as the door closed behind her, he finally realized
a truth he hadn't been willing to acknowledge before.
That he'd never wanted the promotion as much as he
wanted the woman who'd just walked out the door—and
possibly out of his life—forever.

Chapter Fourteen

Gage didn't get much sleep Friday night, and Saturday night wasn't any better. Though he was reluctant to admit it, he'd grown accustomed to sharing his bed with Megan. He would have laughed at anyone who dared to call him a snuggler, but he couldn't deny that he missed the comfort of Megan's warm body next to his.

So he wasn't in the best of moods when he got out of bed Sunday morning, and when he went into the bathroom and saw her toothbrush—the only thing she ever left at his place—his mood grew even dimmer.

He'd suggested that she could bring over some essentials—her own shampoo, body lotion, whatever—but she'd never taken him up on the offer. It was as if she wanted to make sure there was no trace of her presence after she'd gone.

And there was nothing, except for the toothbrush and the aching emptiness inside of him.

He didn't believe that she was gone forever. After all, she was his fiancée, and as upset and angry as she'd been over his deception, she wouldn't break her promise. If he'd learned nothing else about her over the past few months, he'd learned that she was someone who could be counted on.

She was straightforward and honest and loyal, and she deserved a hell of a lot better than someone like him.

She'd pegged him exactly right when she'd said that he didn't let anyone get too close. He'd always been careful to step away from a relationship before either party got too deeply involved.

A wife and a family had never been part of his plan, which was why this relationship with Megan had seemed so perfect. She knew exactly what he wanted. She wasn't supposed to care about him.

And, more importantly, he wasn't supposed to care about her.

But her angry outburst two days earlier, and her absence since then, had given him a lot to think about and a lot of time to think. And he realized that it was time—or maybe past time—for him to make some decisions.

But he was wary of acting impulsively, so he waited until the end of the week to see his father. And all through the week, Megan continued to treat him with the same professional courtesy she'd always demonstrated at work, and she continued to wear his ring on her finger.

She definitely deserved a better deal than the one he'd given her, and on Friday morning, instead of going directly to the research department, Gage headed to the executive wing.

"I was just going over the preliminary trial results for Fedentropin," Allan said when Gage stepped into his office. "It looks like this may be a go even sooner than we anticipated."

Gage nodded. "Megan had pretty high expectations, but even she was impressed by the overwhelmingly positive results."

"And I'm impressed by how well you and Megan have been working together," Allan told him. "I had some concerns initially about your ability to keep your personal relationship separate from your working one, but you both seem to be handling it."

Gage had been looking for an opening, and his father had conveniently dropped it right into his lap. "Actually, that won't be a problem anymore because Megan and I won't be getting married."

Allan frowned. "Why not? What happened?"

He could have told his father that they'd decided to take a break, or that things just didn't work out, but he was determined to finally put an end to all of the lies and deceptions.

"The truth is," he said, "we were never really engaged."

Allan stood up and crossed the room to close his office door. He didn't say anything until he was seated again, and then it was simply, "I'd like an explanation."

So Gage told his father exactly how his engagement with Megan had come to be.

He hated to admit his dishonesty, but he'd realized a couple of things during his confrontation with Megan. The first was that a promotion to the V.P. office wouldn't mean anything if he hadn't earned it on the basis of his work, and the second—and most surprising revelation— was that he didn't even want Dean Garrison's job.

"How did you convince Megan to go along with it?" his father asked when Gage had finished his explanation.

"It wasn't easy," he said, and left it at that. He absolutely was *not* going to tell his father that she'd bartered her compliance with his scam for sexual experience. "But I was persuasive and desperate. I wanted to be vice president, and you made it clear that you would only endorse my candidacy if I could prove I'd changed my ways."

"And you thought getting engaged was the way to do it?"

"It worked, didn't it?"

Allan frowned. "Why are you telling me this now?"

"Because I realized that I don't want the future of my career to be decided on the basis of anything other than my work, and I'm not sure that will ever happen here." His hand wasn't quite steady when he passed the envelope across the desk to his father.

"What's this?" Allan asked, but Gage could tell from the tone of his voice that he already knew.

And though he was certain he was doing the right thing, Gage had to clear his throat before he could respond. "It's my resignation."

"Why?"

"I need to make my own way," he said. "As long as I'm working here, I'll feel like I'm in the shadows of both you and Craig. Maybe I've even hidden in those shadows from time to time, when it suited my purposes, but I don't want to do that anymore."

Allan set the envelope on his desk without opening it. "Is there anything I can say that will make you change your mind?"

Gage shook his head. "You've been waiting for months—" he managed to smile "—or maybe years, for me to grow up. I think I'm finally starting to."

"For what it's worth, I do think your work has demonstrated that you're both capable and deserving of the promotion."

"Thank you."

"I'm sorry that you've decided to leave," his father said. "But I'm also proud of the honesty and courage you've shown in making this decision. And if you ever want to come back, I'll put in a good word with your boss."

Gage's smile came easier this time. "I'll keep that in mind."

"I'm sorry, too, to hear that your relationship with Megan was nothing more than a charade. I really think she could have been good for you."

"She was good for me," Gage said, and knew that it was true.

He wasn't as certain that he'd been good for her, but he wanted to be, if only she would give him the chance.

As difficult as it had been for Gage to tell his father the truth about everything he'd done and everything he was going to do, it was ten times harder to face Megan. But at the end of the day, when they were the only ones left in the lab and would be afforded a degree of privacy, he confided, "I told my father the truth about our relationship."

She looked up from the computer screen where she'd been inputting trial data. "Well, there goes my job security."

"Your job is secure," he assured her. "He doesn't blame you for being dragged into my scheme."

"Is that what you told him?"

"It's the truth, isn't it? You never wanted to be involved in my plan."

But they both knew she had gotten involved, probably more deeply than she'd ever intended, and certainly more deeply than was smart.

"Why now?" she asked him. "Dean will be leaving in a couple of months and—"

"I'm leaving before then," he told her.

She stared at him, uncomprehending.

"I gave my father my resignation today."

"But why? If it's because of what I said last week—"

"It's not," he interrupted. "Or maybe it is, but not for the reasons you think." He smiled wryly. "I'm not self-sacrificing enough to give up something I really want for someone else, but the truth is, I don't really want Dean Garrison's job."

"You don't?"

"I've been working toward the V.P. office for six years," he admitted. "Because it was expected of me, because it was what a Richmond should do. Not because I really wanted it."

She was silent for a long moment before she asked, "What do you want to do?"

"I haven't quite figured that out yet." But he had figured out that he wasn't ready to let go of her, to give up everything they'd shared. "Maybe we could talk about it over dinner?"

She hesitated, then said, "I can't. I'm sorry."

He waited for an explanation, but none was forthcoming.

"Because?" he prompted.

"Because Ashley and Trevor broke up," she finally admitted. "She found out he was fooling around with a woman he works with and called off the wedding."

"Is she okay?"

She seemed surprised that he would ask, and after another momentary hesitation, she responded. "I think so. Or she will be. But in the meantime, my mother heard the news and came home from Switzerland to console her, and Paige and I can't leave her to deal with that alone."

He nodded. "We can do dinner another time."

"Maybe."

She picked up her purse to leave, and paused again while he was still pondering the 'maybe'.

"Good-bye, Gage." She brushed her lips against his, softly, fleetingly. "And good luck. With everything."

Then she turned and walked away, leaving Gage to stare at her retreating form, stunned.

Good-bye?

What the hell was that supposed to mean?

Okay, he knew what the words meant. He'd said them often enough himself at the conclusion of a date or the end of relationship. And maybe that was why they shook him so much—there was something about the way Megan said them that suggested she'd meant them as a final good-bye.

Or maybe it was the kiss—the casual touch of her mouth to his—that warned him she wasn't just walking away. She was already gone.

It was easier for Megan to focus on her sister's heart-break than her own. When Trevor had put his ring on Ashley's finger, they'd been making real plans for their life together. So her sister was more than justified in feeling as if her whole future had been yanked away from her by her lying, cheating fiancé.

In comparison, Megan knew that she had no right to feel betrayed. Gage had never offered her any more than six months and while he'd ended their engagement well short of that mark, he hadn't broken any promises. He'd only ended an illusion.

The knowledge did nothing to lessen the ache in her heart.

She was genuinely pleased for him that he'd decided to end the deception and follow his dreams. And she was grateful that he'd given her the confidence to pursue her own. She was only sorry to realize that somewhere along the way, those dreams had changed.

She'd always been like a fish out of water in social situations, self-conscious about the fact that she faded into the background unnoticed, yet even more uncomfortable if there was any attention focused on her. Gage had helped her overcome her fears and insecurities. It was what she'd wanted, all that she'd expected from their arrangement. It certainly wasn't his fault that she'd fallen in love.

Because now that he was gone, now that their relationship was really and truly over, she could no longer deny that she was in love with Gage Richmond.

Of course, it was a truth she would admit to no one, a heartache she managed to keep buried deep inside only because her sister was too busy nursing her own broken heart to notice that Megan was doing the same. If Paige had any suspicions, she kept them to herself, probably because Lillian's return from Switzerland prevented her from making any mention of the end of an engagement that Lillian had known nothing about.

So Megan was all the more surprised when she came home late from work the following Thursday night and found her mother alone in the kitchen, waiting for her.

"Where's Ashley?"

"She's gone up to bed already."

"Is she okay?"

"As okay as anyone can be after such a betrayal." Lillian gestured to the teapot on the table. "I just made it, if you want a cup."

Megan got a mug from the cupboard and poured before settling in a chair across from her mother. "You never did like Trevor, did you?"

"I didn't dislike him," her mother denied. "I just didn't want Ashley to settle for less than she deserved."

"How did you know that she was?"

"I'm not sure I did know, but I suspected that she didn't love him as much as she'd loved Cameron." Lillian managed a smile. "Of course, a woman rarely loves any other man as much as her first love."

She was obviously thinking of her own first love—her husband and the father of her children. It had always amazed Megan that such love and devotion still existed ten years after Michael Roarke's death, but now it worried her, too. Because if that was true, then she might never love another man as much as she loved Gage Richmond.

"But I think that's something you've learned yourself, isn't it?"

Megan's head shot up. "What?"

Lillian's smile was soft, her eyes filled with understanding. "Did you really think I would look at you and not know that my baby girl had given away her heart?"

The unexpected sympathy was her undoing. Megan's eyes filled with tears. Lillian ran a comforting hand down her back, and the tears spilled over. And suddenly, for the first time, her head was on her mother's shoulder and she was crying her eyes out.

"Do you want to talk about it?" Lillian asked, when her daughter's tears finally stopped.

And Megan realized that she did.

She held nothing back and, when she'd finished, her mother was silent for a moment.

"What are you going to do now?" she finally asked.

"Do?" Megan looked at her blankly. "What can I do? He's the one who decided it was over."

"Did he? Or did he just decide to put an end to the lies?"

"But…I haven't heard anything from him since that day in the lab."

Lillian smiled. "Honey, you spent the better part of the last several months with this man. Surely you've learned something about your own power."

Power? Megan almost laughed out loud. "If you think I have any power over the opposite sex, you must be confusing me with your other daughter."

"I'm not confused at all," her mother denied. "And it's long past time you stopped underestimating yourself."

Had she been doing that? Had she been letting her old fears and insecurities hold her back?

"It's been almost two weeks," she felt compelled to point out. "I'm sure he's forgotten about me by now."

"I doubt that. But if he has, then you need to remind him."

Megan knew it wouldn't be as simple as her mother made it sound, but if there was one thing she knew how to do, it was analyze a problem and figure out a solution. And just the possibility of coming up with a plan made her feel better already, even if she didn't quite know what shape that plan was going to take. "I'm glad you came home, Mom."

Lillian hugged her. "I always will. Anytime you need me."

Megan drew back to look at her. "It sounds like you're planning on leaving again."

"I promised Edward I'd go back as soon as everything was settled here."

"You and Edward—is it serious?"

"I think it might be." A tiny furrow formed between her mother's brows. "Would you be okay with that?"

"You're a grown woman, Mom. You hardly need my permission or approval."

"I know. I guess I just want someone to tell me that it's okay to feel the way I'm feeling."

"You're in love with him?"

"I don't know. But I do know that I have feelings for Edward that I haven't had for any man in a very long time."

"Since Dad?" Megan guessed.

Lillian nodded.

"Are you scared?"

"Terrified," her mother admitted, then laughed. "But at the same time, exhilarated, because I didn't think I ever could feel this way again. For a long time, I wasn't sure I'd ever feel *anything* again."

"You look…happy," Megan decided.

"I am happy," Lillian said. "And that's what I want for you and your sister."

"I think, after what Trevor did, it's going to take some time for Ashley to get there."

"What about you?"

Megan thought about Gage, and suddenly knew what she had to do. And if her mother could put her bruised and battered heart on the line for a second time. Megan could, too.

"I'll keep you posted," she promised.

Gage thought he might enjoy being unemployed for a while, but as it turned out, he was without a job for much less time than he'd anticipated. On Tuesday of the first week after he'd resigned from Richmond Pharmaceuticals, he got a call from a friend who had recently become a major investor in Millhouse, the local microbrewery, and was looking to update and expand.

Brian had been talking about his plans for months, trying to convince Gage to come on board, but Gage had never before taken the offer seriously. This time he did.

He and Brian worked out the details over a couple of beers on Wednesday, and Gage started work on Thursday.

He loved the challenge of the new job, the exploration of new opportunities. And though he was kept busy at work, he was never quite busy enough to prevent thoughts of Megan from sneaking into his mind.

At frequent and unexpected times throughout the day, he would find himself wondering where she was and what she was doing. He wondered about the drug trial and how it was progressing, and if Megan was still putting in a lot of extra hours at the lab. He wondered if she was thinking about him, if she missed him at all, or if she'd already put their relationship out of her mind. And he wondered if she'd started dating other men.

He would bet his first week's salary that Warren Caldwell had hit on her before the week was out. The senior lab tech had started hanging around her at the beginning of the trial, and Megan had honestly believed it was because he was interested in the study.

But Gage knew Warren was checking out more than numbers and patterns, even while Megan was wearing his ring on her finger. Of course, she probably wasn't wearing it anymore, and the absence of the diamond would be a clear signal that Gage was no longer in the picture.

He scowled as he tried to decide whether or not Megan would really go out with someone like Warren. But of course she would. Warren was exactly the kind of mature, responsible man that a woman like Megan would want to settle down with. The thought irritated the hell out of him. Knowing that his irritation was irrational didn't make it any less real.

He was still scowling when the intercom buzzer announced that he had a visitor. A few minutes later, his sister-in-law was at the door.

Tess wasn't in the habit of stopping by unannounced or uninvited and he was understandably wary of her reasons for doing so early on a Saturday morning.

"Let me guess," he said, "you're here to tell me what a mistake I made with Megan?"

"Actually, I came to see how the new job was going."

Though he wasn't sure he believed her, he took the statement at face value and responded. "The job's good. It's a challenge, sometimes even more than I anticipated, and the pay is lousy, but the perks are great."

"Free beer?" she guessed, following him into the kitchen.

"It's a heck of a lot better than a dental plan."

"You obviously don't have a kid who needs braces."

"No kids at all," he reminded her, holding up the coffeepot in silent question.

She nodded. "No kids, no wife, no fiancée."

"And I like it that way."

Tess shook her head as she accepted the mug he gave to her. "And to think that I believed you could actually appreciate a smart, together woman."

Gage slammed his mug onto the counter. "I *knew* that's what this visit was really about, that you came here to give me grief for breaking up with Megan."

"I'm not here to give you grief," she denied. "But since you mentioned it, I'll tell you that I think you did the right thing, even if you did it for the wrong reasons."

"I don't even want to know."

Of course, she ignored him. "You needed to end your relationship with Megan because your desire for her was tied up with your desire for the promotion. Now that you've left the company, it should be easy for you to de-termine exactly what your feelings are."

"I'm relieved," he said.

"Relieved?"

He nodded. "That it ended before anyone developed expectations."

"Hmm." Tess considered this as she lifted her cup, but her tone had the hairs on the back of his neck standing up in a way that warned something big was coming.

"Whose expectations were you worried about? Your parents'? Megan's?" She eyed him over the rim of her mug. "Or your own?"

He laughed. "Come on, Tess. You've known me forever. When have you ever known me to have expectations?"

"Never," she admitted. "Until Megan."

"And what kind of expectations do you think I had?"

She took another sip of her coffee, considering. "I think you started to believe that you and Megan could really make things work. Maybe the engagement was a sham, but as you slipped into the role of soon-to-be groom, you realized it wasn't so bad, and you didn't want it to end."

"You're saying I put an end to the charade because I didn't want it to end?"

"Because you wanted it to be real," she clarified. "Because you fell in love with Meg and didn't want to lose her."

"If that was true," Gage said, playing along. "Why wouldn't I say 'I love you, Meg, let's make this fake en-gagement real'?"

"Because you didn't believe that she would stay," she said. Then, more gently, "Because the women in your life never do. Do they, Gage? Not even your mother."

He scowled, no longer amused.

"And since then, anytime someone gets a little too close, you push her away."

"You're reading far too much into this," he said. "Megan and I both knew from the beginning that the arrangement was only temporary."

"I'm telling you what I see," his sister-in-law said. "Because I've seen it before. Because I went through the same thing with your brother."

He remembered, vaguely, that Craig and Tess had gone through some rocky times early in their marriage, but he wasn't privy to all of the details—nor did he want to be.

She finished her coffee and looked him in the eye. "And because I know that if you let her go, you'll regret it for the rest of your life."

Chapter Fifteen

Almost three weeks after Gage had ended their engagement, and a week after the unexpected heart-to-heart with her mother, Megan finally had a plan. It wasn't a particularly complicated or innovative plan, she was simply going to face Gage and confess her true feelings.

If he didn't feel the same way about her, well, there was nothing she could do about that. But she couldn't let everything they'd started to build together just fall apart because she was too cowardly to put her heart on the line.

Gage wasn't Darrin Walsh or Sam Meyer or Bill Penske. He was his own person, something he'd proved to everyone by walking away from the security of Richmond Pharmaceuticals to follow his own dreams. And he was an incredible man, a man who had made her believe she was worthy of being loved. The only question now was—could *he* love her?

Once she'd made up her mind to find that out, she didn't let herself vacillate but went directly to his condo after work on Wednesday.

She caught the door as one of the tenants was leaving so Gage didn't have to buzz her into the building. And since he didn't know she was there, she could still change her mind and walk out again. A distinct possibility as she was having serious doubts about whether she could go through with her plan.

It's long past time you stopped underestimating yourself.

Bolstered by her mother's words, Megan lifted her hand to knock.

Before she even had a chance to catch her breath, the door opened and he was there. He hadn't changed at all in the three weeks they'd been apart, nor had his effect on her diminished. Her pulse pounded and her heart ached.

"Megan."

Was it longing she heard in his voice—or was she just imagining it?

"Hi," she said. "I know I should have called—"

"No," he interrupted quickly. "You didn't need to call. It's good to see you."

His eyes roamed over her, skimming from head to toe, as if maybe he'd missed her as much as she'd missed him.

"Can I come in?"

"Oh. Yeah. Sure." He stepped away from the door so that she could enter.

She went down the hall to the kitchen, more out of habit than purpose. She didn't sit down but stood behind one of the high-back chairs, her fingers curled around the wood.

"Can I get you anything? Coffee? A glass of wine?"

She shook her head. "No, thanks. I really didn't plan on staying long, I just wanted to clear up a few things."

"What things?"

He hadn't swept her into his arms and declared his undying love, and maybe she'd been foolish enough to hope the scene would play out that way so that she didn't have to be the one to put her heart on the line. But she wouldn't have come here if she hadn't been prepared to risk everything, if she hadn't believed the potential reward was worth everything.

"For starters, I wanted to return this." She took the ring out of her pocket and set it on the table.

He stared at the diamond cluster for a long moment. "It's yours," he finally said. "Remember—you were going to hock it and pay off your mortgage?"

She managed a smile. "Well, things didn't quite go according to plan, did they?"

He held her gaze for a long moment. "No, they didn't."

"I also want to apologize."

"What do you have to apologize for?"

"The last time I was here, I jumped all over you for lying to me about the reasons for our fake engagement. But I lied to you, too," she admitted. "When I told you that I wanted to learn how to talk to and flirt with other men, it was a lie—even if I didn't realize it at the time. Because from the first moment I walked into Richmond Pharmaceuticals, I only wanted you. And the more I got to know you, the more I wanted you.

"But you didn't even seem to know I existed until that day at the mall. And then I found out that the only reason you noticed me then was because I was completely different from every other woman you'd ever dated."

"You *are* different," he told her. "But in all the very best ways."

"You made me believe that. You helped me believe in me…and to believe in us." She took a deep breath, then forged ahead. "I didn't go into this expecting to fall in love with you. In fact, it was the absolute last thing I wanted to happen. But it happened anyway. I love you, Gage."

She was looking at him when she said it, and though she wasn't surprised by the panic that came into his eyes, she was disappointed.

He swallowed. "Don't you think you're jumping ahead here a little?"

"No, I don't. But I am taking a leap of faith, trusting that I wouldn't have fallen so completely for a man who isn't capable of feeling the same way.

"When you ended our phony engagement, I thought it was because you didn't need me," she told him. "Because you'd figured out what you wanted and you no longer needed to be with me to help you get it.

"It was only after you'd gone, after I'd had some time to get over the shock of everything ending so abruptly, that I really thought about what you'd said. And I realized that you needed me a lot more than you were willing to admit, even to yourself."

"That's an interesting theory," he said. "But I'm not sure it's anything more than that."

His words, and the dismissal inherent in them, hurt, but she knew that was his intent, his way of distracting her because she was getting too close to the truth. Because she'd gotten too close to the barriers he'd carefully erected around his heart. She still didn't know why they were there, what had happened to make him so reluctant to open up to anyone, but she wasn't ready to give up on him yet.

"You told me that you weren't self-sacrificing enough to give up something you really want for someone else," she reminded him. "But I think you would give up something you wanted rather than admit how much you wanted it. Because somewhere along the line you lost someone who really mattered, and you decided not to let anyone else ever matter that much again."

"You think you have it all figured out, don't you?"

"No, I don't," she denied softly. "But I think we could figure it out together."

"You don't know what you're talking about. You don't have a clue."

She heard the pain in his voice now, the raw edge he wasn't quite able to bury beneath the scorn.

"Maybe not. But I do know what I'm asking. I'm asking you to put your heart on the line and trust me. To give us a real chance to make this work."

But Gage didn't say anything else, and Megan finally left his condo with her heart and her hopes in pieces.

Three days after Megan's visit, the ring she'd left was still sitting in the center of his kitchen table. The platinum glinted in the sunlight that streamed through the window, the cluster of diamonds dazzled. But Gage knew it was nothing more than a band of metal and some hunks of carbon. Surely it shouldn't have had the power to change his life.

And it hadn't, not at first. When he'd bought the ring for Megan, when he'd put it on her finger, there had been no promises of love or dreams of happily ever after. It had been a symbol to the rest of the world. It hadn't really meant anything to him.

But somehow putting the ring on Megan's finger,

even under false pretenses, had changed his life. Because the action had made her a part of it.

And then she'd taken the ring off, and he'd watched her walk away. He'd wanted so desperately to hold on to her, but he'd let her go because he was afraid to risk his heart, to lose someone he loved all over again. And yet that was exactly what had happened.

Now the ring that had once meant nothing to him meant everything, because it was a symbol of everything he'd had and lost.

You would give up something you wanted rather than admit how much you wanted it.

Maybe there had been some truth in her words, but not anymore.

He snatched the ring off of the table and headed for the door.

Sunday brunch with Ashley and Paige promised to be the one bright light in what had been an otherwise dismal and depressing week for Megan.

She'd thought it would get easier. She'd honestly believed that with each day that passed, she would miss Gage a little bit less until she stopped thinking about him altogether. Instead, the aching emptiness inside seemed to grow a little bit bigger each day.

But she looked forward to brunch because it was time with her sister and her cousin, and because she was sure they could keep her from thinking about Gage, at least for a while. And that seemed cause enough for a celebration, so she ordered the mimosas this time.

"I'm not in the mood for champagne," Ashley said.

Though her sister had traded in the yoga pants and T-shirts that had become her household attire for a simple sheath-style dress in a pretty sage-green color, the recent loss of ten pounds was apparent in the way the garment hung on her frame, and no amount of makeup could disguise the shadows under her eyes.

"You should be jumping for joy," Paige told her.

"Why?" Ashley asked the question that was expected, though her tone revealed a distinct lack of interest in the response.

"Because you found out your fiancé was screwing around before you made the mistake of marrying him."

"Is that supposed to make me feel better—knowing the man who claimed to love me was bored with me even before the wedding?" Ashley's eyes filled with tears. "Because it doesn't. And even if he was a two-timing snake, he was going to be the father of my children. Now I'll never have a baby of my own."

Megan touched her sister's hand. "You will. You just have to be patient."

"How can I be patient when I know my time is running out?"

"If you really think your time is running out, go to a sperm bank," Paige suggested. "An injection is more dependable than a man."

"A sperm bank?" Apparently Ashley had never considered the possibility. Of course, there had been no reason to consider such an option while she'd been planning to marry Trevor, but she was obviously giving it some thought now.

Megan shot Paige a look, silently reproaching her for dangling the possibility in front of her sister like a baited fish hook, especially when Ashley was feeling so vulnerable and desperate.

"Can we forget about Trevor for now?" Megan suggested. "In fact, let's not talk about men at all today."

"We can definitely forget about Trevor," Ashley said.

"And we can not talk about men," Paige agreed. "As soon as we find out why you returned that big hunk of rock."

"Because the ring was never really mine any more than Gage was mine."

"But I thought it was part of the agreement that you got to keep the diamonds."

She shrugged, as if it was no big deal. "It was, but after all was said and done, it just didn't feel right."

Ashley tossed back the champagne she claimed she hadn't wanted. "Like the scene in *Pretty Woman* when Julia Roberts walks out of Richard Gere's hotel room without the money he tossed on the bed."

"Thanks for comparing me to a prostitute," Megan said. Paige chuckled.

"She left the money because she cared about him, because she didn't want to be a prostitute to him," her sister said staunchly. "And you gave back Gage's ring because you didn't want to be his fiancée-for-hire. You only wanted it if it was for real."

Megan picked up her champagne glass and studied the rising bubbles. "I never had any illusions that it could be real."

"I did." Paige's admission surprised both of her cousins; she shrugged. "I know you think I'm the cynical one—"

"You are the cynical one," Ashley asserted, then sighed. "But more often than not, you're the right one, too."

Paige waved off her comment. "But the first time I saw Megan and Gage together, they just seemed to fit. And I hoped—regardless of their own reasons for agreeing to the fake engagement—they would both realize they belonged together."

"I thought they belonged together, too," Ashley said.

"I thought we were not talking about men today," Megan reminded them both.

"Okay, we can stop talking about Gage. But not talking about him isn't going to help you stop thinking about him," Paige warned.

Of course, Megan knew that already.

After brunch, when she pulled into her driveway at home, Megan worried that it was the prevalence of Gage in her thoughts that made her imagine he was standing on her porch.

But when she got out of her car, he was still there.

She kept her pace steady as she made her way up the walk, even while her heart was pounding against her ribs and her eyes were devouring him.

He was casually dressed in a pair of khakis and a short-sleeved, Henley-style shirt, and there was a light shadow of stubble on his jaw because he didn't shave on Sundays. She'd only once complained about the roughness of his unshaven cheeks, and then he'd shown her that the contrast of his rough beard against her tender skin could be incredibly erotic.

Definitely *not* a memory she should be indulging in at the moment.

She drew in a deep breath, exhaled it slowly and tried to play it casual. "Hello, Gage."

"Hi." He offered her the armful of flowers she hadn't even realized he was holding. "I brought these for you."

She looked down at the gorgeous array of tulips and daffodils and irises and daisies. "They're beautiful," she said, "but…why are you giving me flowers?"

"Because they're spring flowers."

She didn't see how his response answered her question, but she took the bouquet, anyway. "Thank you." She dug her keys out of her pocket. "I'll go put them in some water."

Gage cleared his throat. "Can I come in?"

She would have expected he would just walk through the door if he wanted to come in. That he'd bothered to ask suggested he might be feeling as uncertain as Megan at the moment.

"Sure," she said, and he followed her through the door.

"I don't have any beer," she told him. "But I could put on a pot of coffee."

"I'll do it," he said. "You take care of the flowers."

So he made the coffee while she arranged the blooms and tried not to think about how much she'd missed him and how thrilled she was that he was in her kitchen, even if all he wanted from her was a cup of coffee.

"There are even crocuses in here," she noted, shifting some of the stems to balance the colors in the arrangement.

"What are crocuses?"

She smiled as she pointed. "The purple ones with the yellow centers."

"Are they spring flowers, too?"

She nodded.

"I told the florist I wanted all spring flowers," he explained. "Because I remembered that they were your favorites, because you said spring is a time of reawakening, when anything is possible. And because I needed to believe that what I want is possible."

She set the vase carefully in the center of the table. Her heart was pounding so loudly now she was surprised he couldn't hear it, but she managed to keep her voice level when she asked, "What do you want, Gage?"

"I want a second chance. For us."

She didn't know what had happened to change his mind, and she was afraid to let herself believe that he really had.

"We never had a first chance," she reminded him. "What we had was an arrangement, an illusion. None of it was real."

"It *was* real," he told her. "More real than I wanted to admit, because then I would have to admit that my feelings for you were real. When you walked out on me—"

"Me?" She hadn't intended to interrupt, but she couldn't let the accusation pass without comment. "I told you I loved you."

"I know. And then you walked out…just like my mother walked out."

That caught her by surprise, and answered so many questions.

"How old were you?" she asked softly.

"Only a few months, the first time."

"How many times were there?"

"I honestly don't know." He turned to pour himself a cup of coffee that she suspected he didn't want half as much as he wanted something to do, somewhere to focus his attention while he spoke about things he'd probably never spoken about before. "I don't have a lot of memories of her being there, but I know that she was, then she was gone."

"And you were a helpless, bewildered child who had everything yanked away from him."

He shook his head. "Don't feel sorry for me. It wasn't like that. I wasn't abandoned or alone. My dad was there. He was always there for us."

"I don't feel sorry for you," she said. "I feel sorry for the child you were, and maybe now I understand a little bit more why you always held yourself back, but I don't feel sorry for you."

"I didn't always hold myself back. I tried to," he admitted. "But I couldn't hold out against you."

"You gave a pretty good impression."

He shrugged. "Years of experience. But even with so much practice keeping my emotions in check, you got under my skin.

"All along I've made mistakes, miscalculations, mostly because I assumed that you were like other women. That you were like Beth."

"Who's Beth?"

"No one important," he said dismissively.

"She's important if you thought I was like her."

"I was wrong."

"You loved her," she guessed.

He sighed. "I thought I did. And I thought she loved me. It turned out that she loved the Richmond fortune."

Megan folded her arms across her chest. "I never wanted your money."

"I know—you wanted my body."

She couldn't deny that, and Gage's smile assured her that he had no objection to the fact.

"But that wasn't why I knew you were different. And it wasn't until you were gone that I finally realized what truly set you apart from anyone else I've ever known— and that's the way I feel about you.

"At the end of any other relationship, I've usually only felt relief. I was never looking for anything long-term. And then you came along and without even realizing what was happening, everything changed for me.

"I looked forward to coming to the lab every day, not because of the challenges the work presented but because I'd get to see you. And sometimes, if I was lucky enough to catch your eye, you'd give me one of those little smiles, and I'd feel as if I could conquer the world.

"I didn't want a relationship, I wanted a promotion. But somehow, I started thinking beyond my career, and you were at the center of all those thoughts, and that scared the hell out of me."

She wasn't sure she'd ever heard him make such a speech. She was sure that he'd never been so open about his feelings. And as she listened to him confess to fears so similar to her own, she began to hope.

"And it wasn't just that I wanted *you,*" he told her. "It was that you made me look at my life and think about my dreams. You made me realize that I wanted more, and you made me want to be a better person—someone who might be worthy of you.

"I'm not there yet," he admitted. "But I've made a start. I know it's early days still, but I'm enjoying my new job, and knowing that I will succeed or fail on the merits of my efforts. And I'm confident that I will succeed, because another thing I've realized is that I have ambition and pride and I won't accept any less than 100 percent from myself—at my job or in my personal life."

She'd known that about him already. But she hadn't dared let herself believe that he could be so committed to her. And even now, even listening to his words and hearing the emotion in his voice, there was still a part of her that was afraid to trust in what he was saying.

"I've never been all the way in love before," he told her.

Her heart stuttered in response to the implications that he could be all the way in love now—with her. "I certainly never gave a relationship my complete focus or attention," he continued. "Because I was scared. You were right about that. After my experience with Beth, I was even more cautious. I was afraid that if I let myself love someone, I would be hurt.

"But I've realized there's something that scares me more than opening up my heart—and that's the possibility of losing you forever. And that's why I'm here— to tell you that I love you, to give you 100 percent of my heart, and to assure you that if you're willing to take a chance on me, I will do my damnedest to ensure you never regret it."

He loved her. Her mind spun, her heart soared. She wanted to throw her arms around him and tell him that she loved him, too, but she only said, "Do you realize that you told me more about yourself in the past ten minutes than you did during the entire course of our fake engagement?"

"Was it too much? Did I scare you off?"

She shook her head. "It wasn't too much, and I don't scare easily."

"You used to tremble when I kissed you."

Her lips curved. "Not because I was scared."

He lifted a brow, then tipped her chin up with his finger and brushed his lips against hers. Softly. Sweetly. Longingly.

She trembled; he smiled.

"I missed you," he said, and with those words, the scattered pieces of her broken heart began to reassemble.

"I missed you, too," she admitted.

"I love you, Megan."

And the jagged edges of those broken pieces knitted together, and her heart swelled until it filled her whole chest.

"I love you, too."

His arms tightened around her. "Do you love me enough to make it for real this time?"

She swallowed. "Make what real?"

"Our engagement."

She stepped back, shocked. "Do you really mean it?"

"I really mean it," he assured her. "In fact, I've got the ring to prove it."

He pulled the box out of his pocket.

Her breath hitched when she recognized The Diamond Jubilee logo on the top. Then he flipped open the lid, and her eyes filled with tears.

"That's not my ring."

"It is if you want it."

If she wanted it? There wasn't anything she wanted more. But she had to ask, "What happened to the other one?"

"I took it back," he told her. "Aside from the fact that you never wanted that ring, I didn't want you wearing a ring that had symbolized a false promise."

Instead he'd chosen a modest round cut diamond set on a simple gold band—the exact ring she'd originally picked out.

"Does this prove that I'm serious?" he asked.

She nodded, her throat too tight to speak, her newly healed heart pounding hard and fast.

"This time, it's just about us," he told her. "I have no ulterior motives or secret agendas. I've finally realized what I want, and more than anything, what I want is to spend my life with you."

"I always knew what I wanted," she told him. "Even if I wasn't willing to admit it. And what I want is to spend my life with you."

He slid the ring onto her finger. "Do you remember how we were going to tell your mother that we wanted a long engagement?"

She nodded.

"Well, I don't want a long engagement," he warned her.

"You want to be married before next year's most desirable bachelors list is published, don't you?" she teased.

"Way before then." He wrapped his arms around her, held her tight.

She snuggled into his embrace and smiled, secure in his arms and in the knowledge that she'd finally found where she belonged.

Epilogue

Three days later, after a quick, simple ceremony, Megan and Gage walked out of the courthouse, hand in hand.

They were followed by her mother and Ashley and Paige and his parents and Craig and Tess and their four kids. While Megan couldn't—in good conscience— get married without her family around her, she knew she would go insane if she let her mother plan a big, fancy wedding. Instead, she'd put Lillian in charge of setting up an intimate family dinner to celebrate the occasion, and her mother had happily made the arrangements.

Other than Lillian, Megan's biggest concern had been Ashley's response to the hasty nuptials, because she knew her sister was still hurting over her own broken engagement. But Ashley was genuinely thrilled to witness the union, though she did take Gage aside beforehand to warn that he would answer to her if he ever did anything to dim the stars in her sister's eyes. Gage assured her that he wouldn't, and because she could see the same stars in his, Ashley believed him.

But the biggest surprise had been seeing Paige wipe tears from her cheeks after the ceremony. Of course, Megan had always suspected that her cousin was the biggest romantic of them all, and she sent up a silent prayer that both Ashley and Paige would someday find partners who made them as happy as Gage made her.

As if he could read her thoughts, Gage squeezed her hand gently. The hand on which she now wore a simple gold band nestled against her new engagement ring.

She looked up at him and smiled. "I still can't believe it—first we were engaged, then we weren't, and now we're married."

"Are you sorry that we did it so fast instead of having a big fancy wedding?"

She shook her head emphatically. "Definitely not. And now we can move straight to the honeymoon."

"I would like nothing more than to take you away to somewhere with lots of sunshine and warm, sandy beaches, but I can hardly ask for a couple weeks off from a job I only started a couple weeks ago."

"I don't need to go anywhere," she assured him. "I just need to be with you."

"In that case, I've got a plan."

"I'm not sure I like the sound of that. The last time you came up with a plan, it was about a fake engagement."

"You'll like this one," he promised.

"What does it involve?"

"Just you and me, a long weekend and the keys to the house in Lake Placid."

"I think I do like that one." She wrapped her arms around him. "In fact, it sounds like an absolutely perfect plan."

* * * * *

Don't miss THE PREGNANCY PLAN
the next book in Brenda Harlen's
new Special Edition miniseries
BRIDES & BABIES
on sale in April 2010,
wherever Silhouette books are sold.

*Fan favorite Leslie Kelly is bringing her
readers a fantasy so scandalous,
we're calling it FORBIDDEN!*

*Look for
PLAY WITH ME
Available February 2010
from Harlequin® Blaze™.*

"AREN'T YOU GOING TO SAY 'Fly me' or at least 'Welcome Aboard'?"

Amanda Bauer didn't. The softly muttered word that actually came out of her mouth was a lot less welcoming. And had fewer letters. Four, to be exact.

The man shook his head and tsked. "Not exactly the friendly skies. Haven't caught the spirit yet this morning?"

"Make one more airline-slogan crack and you'll be walking to Chicago," she said.

He nodded once, then pushed his sunglasses onto the top of his tousled hair. The move revealed blue eyes that matched the sky above. And yeah. They were twinkling. Dammit.

"Understood. Just, uh, promise me you'll say 'Coffee, tea or me' at least once, okay? Please?"

Amanda tried to glare, but that twinkle sucked the annoyance right out of her. She could only draw in a slow breath as he climbed into the plane. As she watched her passenger disappear into the small jet, she had to wonder about the trip she was about to take.

Coffee and tea they had, and he was welcome to them. But her? Well, she'd never even considered making a move on a customer before. Talk about unprofessional.

And yet…

Something inside her suddenly wanted to take a chance, to be a little outrageous.

How long since she had done indecent things—or decent ones, for that matter—with a sexy man? Not since before they'd thrown all their energies into expanding Clear-Blue Air, at the very least. She hadn't had time for a lunch date, much less the kind of lust-fest she'd enjoyed in her younger years. The kind that lasted for entire weekends and involved not leaving a bed except to grab the kind of sensuous food that could be smeared onto—and eaten off—someone else's hot, naked, sweat-tinged body.

She closed her eyes, her hand clenching tight on the railing. Her heart fluttered in her chest and she tried to make herself move. But she couldn't—not climbing up, but not backing away, either. Not physically, and not in her head.

Was she really considering this? God, she hadn't even looked at the stranger's left hand to make sure he was available. She had no idea if he was actually attracted to her or just an irrepressible flirt. Yet something inside was telling her to take a shot with this man.

It was crazy. Something she'd never considered. Yet right now, at this moment, she was definitely considering it. If he was available…could she do it? Seduce a stranger. Have an anonymous fling, like something out of a blue movie on late-night cable?

She didn't know. All she knew was that the flight to Chicago was a short one so she had to decide quickly. And as she put her foot on the bottom step and began to climb up, Amanda suddenly had to wonder if she was about to embark on the ride of her life.

Sold, bought, bargained for or bartered

He'll take his...

Bride on Approval

Whether there's a debt to be paid,
a will to be obeyed or a business
to be saved...she has no choice
but to say, "I do"!

PURE PRINCESS,
BARTERED BRIDE
by *Caitlin Crews*
#2894

Available February 2010!

HARLEQUIN
Ambassadors

Want to share your passion for reading Harlequin® Books?

Become a Harlequin Ambassador!

Harlequin Ambassadors are a group of passionate and well-connected readers who are willing to share their joy of reading Harlequin® books with family and friends.

You'll be sent all the tools you need to spark great conversation, including free books!

All we ask is that you share the romance with your friends and family!

You'll also be invited to have a say in new book ideas and exchange opinions with women just like you!

To see if you qualify* to be a Harlequin Ambassador, please visit www.HarlequinAmbassadors.com.

*Please note that not everyone who applies to be a Harlequin Ambassador will qualify. For more information please visit www.HarlequinAmbassadors.com.

Thank you for your participation.

REQUEST YOUR FREE BOOKS!

2 FREE NOVELS PLUS 2 FREE GIFTS!

SPECIAL EDITION

Life, Love and Family!

YES! Please send me 2 FREE Silhouette® Special Edition® novels and my 2 FREE gifts (gifts are worth about $10). After receiving them, if I don't wish to receive any more books, I can return the shipping statement marked "cancel." If I don't cancel, I will receive 6 brand-new novels every month and be billed just $4.24 per book in the U.S. or $4.99 per book in Canada. That's a saving of 15% off the cover price! It's quite a bargain! Shipping and handling is just 50¢ per book in the U.S. and 75¢ per book in Canada.* I understand that accepting the 2 free books and gifts places me under no obligation to buy anything. I can always return a shipment and cancel at any time. Even if I never buy another book from Silhouette, the two free books and gifts are mine to keep forever.

235 SDN E4NC   335 SDN E4NN

_____
Name   (PLEASE PRINT)

_____
Address   Apt. #

_____
City   State/Prov.   Zip/Postal Code

_____
Signature (if under 18, a parent or guardian must sign)

Mail to the **Silhouette Reader Service:**
IN U.S.A.: P.O. Box 1867, Buffalo, NY 14240-1867
IN CANADA: P.O. Box 609, Fort Erie, Ontario L2A 5X3

Not valid for current subscribers to Silhouette Special Edition books.

Want to try two free books from another line?
Call 1-800-873-8635 or visit www.morefreebooks.com.

* Terms and prices subject to change without notice. Prices do not include applicable taxes. N.Y. residents add applicable sales tax. Canadian residents will be charged applicable provincial taxes and GST. Offer not valid in Quebec. This offer is limited to one order per household. All orders subject to approval. Credit or debit balances in a customer's account(s) may be offset by any other outstanding balance owed by or to the customer. Please allow 4 to 6 weeks for delivery. Offer available while quantities last.

Your Privacy: Silhouette is committed to protecting your privacy. Our Privacy Policy is available online at www.eHarlequin.com or upon request from the Reader Service. From time to time we make our lists of customers available to reputable third parties who may have a product or service of interest to you. If you would prefer we not share your name and address, please check here. ☐

Help us get it right—We strive for accurate, respectful and relevant communications. To clarify or modify your communication preferences, visit us at www.ReaderService.com/consumerchoice.

SSE10